The Inn at Holiday Bay:
Boxes in the Basement

by

Kathi Daley

I want to thank the very talented Jessica Fischer for the cover art.

I so appreciate Bruce Curran, who is always ready and willing to answer my cyber questions; Jayme Maness for helping out with the book clubs; and Peggy Hyndman for helping sleuth out those pesky typos.

And, of course, thanks to the readers and bloggers in my life, who make doing what I do possible.

Thank you to Randy Ladenheim-Gil for the editing.

And finally, I want to thank my husband Ken for allowing me time to write by taking care of everything else.

Books by Kathi Daley

Come for the murder, stay for the romance

Zoe Donovan Cozy Mystery:

Halloween Hijinks
The Trouble With Turkeys
Christmas Crazy
Cupid's Curse
Big Bunny Bump-off
Beach Blanket Barbie
Maui Madness
Derby Divas
Haunted Hamlet
Turkeys, Tuxes, and Tabbies
Christmas Cozy
Alaskan Alliance
Matrimony Meltdown
Soul Surrender
Heavenly Honeymoon
Hopscotch Homicide
Ghostly Graveyard
Santa Sleuth
Shamrock Shenanigans
Kitten Kaboodle
Costume Catastrophe
Candy Cane Caper
Holiday Hangover
Easter Escapade
Camp Carter
Trick or Treason
Reindeer Roundup
Hippity Hoppity Homicide
Firework Fiasco

Henderson House
Holiday Hostage – *December 2018*

Zimmerman Academy The New Normal
Zimmerman Academy New Beginnings
Ashton Falls Cozy Cookbook

Tj Jensen Paradise Lake Mysteries by Henery Press:

Pumpkins in Paradise
Snowmen in Paradise
Bikinis in Paradise
Christmas in Paradise
Puppies in Paradise
Halloween in Paradise
Treasure in Paradise
Fireworks in Paradise
Beaches in Paradise
Thanksgiving in Paradise – *Fall 2019*

Whales and Tails Cozy Mystery:

Romeow and Juliet
The Mad Catter
Grimm's Furry Tail
Much Ado About Felines
Legend of Tabby Hollow
Cat of Christmas Past
A Tale of Two Tabbies
The Great Catsby
Count Catula
The Cat of Christmas Present
A Winter's Tail
The Taming of the Tabby

Frankencat
The Cat of Christmas Future
Farewell to Felines
A Whisker in Time
The Catsgiving Feast
A Whale of a Tail – *April 2019*

Writers' Retreat Southern Seashore Mystery:
First Case
Second Look
Third Strike
Fourth Victim
Fifth Night
Sixth Cabin
Seventh Chapter
Eighth Witness – *January 2019*

Rescue Alaska Paranormal Mystery:
Finding Justice
Finding Answers
Finding Courage
Finding Christmas – *December 2018*

A Tess and Tilly Mystery:
The Christmas Letter
The Valentine Mystery
The Mother's Day Mishap
The Halloween House
The Thanksgiving Trip
The Saint Paddy's Promise – *March 2019*

The Inn at Holiday Bay:
Boxes in the Basement
Letters in the Library – *February 2019*

Family Ties:
The Hathaway Sisters
Harper – *February 2019*
Harlow – *May 2019*
Haden – *August 2019*
Haley – *November 2019*

Haunting by the Sea:
Homecoming by the Sea
Secrets by the Sea
Missing by the Sea
Christmas by the Sea – *March 2019*

Sand and Sea Hawaiian Mystery:
Murder at Dolphin Bay
Murder at Sunrise Beach
Murder at the Witching Hour
Murder at Christmas
Murder at Turtle Cove
Murder at Water's Edge
Murder at Midnight

Seacliff High Mystery:
The Secret
The Curse
The Relic
The Conspiracy

The Grudge
The Shadow
The Haunting

Road to Christmas Romance:
Road to Christmas Past

Chapter 1

Maybe it *had* been insanity that caused me to sell my condo, pack my belongings, and buy a huge old house I had never even seen. Maybe it *had* been my unwillingness to face the grief I *would* not deal with and *could* not escape, that caused me to move to a town I knew nothing about and had never even visited. Or maybe, just maybe, when I'd seen the ad for the rundown old house perched on a bluff overlooking the sea, I hadn't been running at all. Maybe, I tried desperately to convince myself, I'd simply seen the opportunity to do something fun. Creative. Different.

No, I admitted as I gingerly placed a foot on the first of three rotted steps leading to the decayed front porch. It hadn't been insanity, an unwillingness to deal, or a longing for fun that caused me to give up my life in California to move to a tiny town in coastal Maine where no one knew who I was or what I had been through. What it had been, I decided, was preservation.

I sighed in relief when I made it to the front door without falling through the rotted wood. I took out the brand-new key I'd been given by the Realtor after he'd had the locks changed prior to my arrival, opened the door, and then stepped into the entry. The floor was damaged and would need to be replaced, and the wallpaper was peeling and would need to be stripped, but the rooms were totally empty, and empty rooms, I knew, even those in disrepair, were preferable to rooms filled with well-meaning friends who were unable to deal with your grief and wanted to help but felt helpless to do so.

The entrance to the home was large and airy and opened up to twin staircases spiraling toward the second story. I'd been told the house had three stories of living space, ten bedrooms, eight baths, and a large living area consisting of several rooms including a parlor and a library, on the first floor. I was also promised the property included a separate guesthouse that could be used as a mother-in-law unit. Apparently, the English gentleman who built the house back in 1895 had grand plans to marry his one true love and fill those ten bedrooms with chubby-cheeked children, but his dream, like mine, had never come to fruition, and so like me, he'd moved away. I knew there had been several owners between Chamberlain Westminster and Bodine Devine, the man from whom I'd bought the house. I wasn't certain of the entire history, but I supposed it didn't really matter.

While my move to the small town of Holiday Bay might not have been well-thought-out, the challenge to gently nudge the old girl back to her former glory had come at the perfect time. The house, I decided, would occupy my energy and my mind. Rehabilitating it would give me focus and provide a safe harbor from which I could fight my demons and finally begin to heal.

My long brown hair blew across my face as the front door blew open behind me. I whirled around, prepared to defend my territory, but all I found was empty space. I put a hand to my chest as my heart pounded. There was no one there; it was just the wind. I had to admit this huge, empty house had me on edge. It was almost as if I was half-expecting someone or something to jump out at me from around every corner. I took a deep breath, crossed the room, and reached for the door, preparing to remedy the situation, when a huge orange cat that had to be half mountain lion given its enormous size, darted between my legs and into the entry. "Shoo," I said as I waved my arms toward it. The cat looked at me with eyes as green as my own, took a few steps, turned, then trotted up the stairs. "Hey," I called after the feline. "You don't live here. You really can't stay." The cat reached the landing at the top of the first flight of stairs, turned to glare at me once again, and then continued down the hallway.

"Damn cat," I muttered under my breath. Life, I decided, was a cruel jokester. As if I didn't have enough to deal with, I now seemed to have a stowaway. Suffice it to say, Abby Sullivan was not now, nor had she ever been, a cat person, or any kind of animal person for that matter. I considered going after the cat but decided that perhaps it would find its way out on its own.

Returning my attention to the house, I walked into what, I assumed, was the main living area. The room was empty, but the hand-carved mantel, which framed the old stone fireplace, truly was a work of art. I ran my hand over the intricately carved surface and imagined the craftsman who had taken the time to get every detail just right. Hand carvings like this were rare these days, and I knew in my heart that the mantel, at least, would need to be preserved.

I turned back toward the room and considered the intricately carved crown molding along the ceiling. There were sections that would need to be replaced, but I supposed the damaged sections could be replicated. It would be a shame to tear down the original material if there was any way it could be saved.

I knew I'd taken on a project when I bought the place, but until I'd arrived and had a chance to look around, I'd had no idea how truly large a project it would be. There were a lot of rooms in need of attention, and so far it looked as if each room was the size of my entire condo back in San Francisco.

No need to panic, I assured myself, as I walked into the room I assumed had been previously used as a formal dining area. The house was going to be a lot of work, but I was up for the task. I'd just need to get organized, consider the entire project, and come up with a plan. From my experience, almost any project was possible as long as I broke it down into small steps I could handle so I wouldn't be overwhelmed by the magnitude of the work in its entirety.

I walked through the dining area to the back of the house, where I imagined I'd find the kitchen. The room was charming in an old-fashioned way. It was a large room with a lot of potential, although the appliances were ancient, the wallpaper peeling, and the cabinets dated. I supposed a total gut job would be required for this particular room, which meant that a hotplate and microwave might be good items to purchase, along with cleaning supplies, mousetraps, and maybe something that would provide the mountain lion, who I was certain was still prowling around upstairs, motivation to leave. What I needed, I realized, was a list. I took out my phone and opened an app. Taking action, any action, seemed like a move in a positive direction, which provided my slightly overwhelmed psyche with the illusion of control.

"Number one," I said aloud, "go to the store and buy food to last several days, and maybe an ice chest to store the food until the status of the refrigerator can be determined."

I walked over to the refrigerator and opened the door. I grimaced at the mess I found and then took a step back. Determining status didn't seem to be the issue so much as replacing the old unit with something less disgusting.

"Number two," I continued, as I walked around the room, opening and closing cupboards, "find a place to set up a home base while renovations are underway." I had brought an air mattress, sleeping bag, pillow, and jug of water with me, so once I'd figured out where to set up, I'd bring it all in and build a little nest. I had a stack of books, several bottles of wine, music on my phone, and even a propane light that would come in handy until I could deal with the electricity.

"Number three," I said into my phone, "have gas, water, and electricity turned on." I paused and looked around at the shabby interior. It really had been a while since the house had been lived in. "Number four," I added, "find a plumber and an electrician to check everything out before using the gas, water, and electricity."

There was a door leading off the kitchen that I assumed led to the basement that had been part of the listing. I turned the handle and opened the door to find wooden stairs descending into a dark space. Closing the door, I decided to leave a tour of the basement for another time and continued toward the rear of the house. The laundry area was large, but the windows had been boarded up, and the place was nothing more than a tangle of cobwebs. Taking a deep breath, I continued to the back door, which led out onto a huge deck that actually appeared to be in good repair. Climbing down from the deck, I headed in the direction of an adorable little cottage the Realtor had referred to as the guesthouse. From its location on the edge of the sea, I bet the view from this little place would probably be even more spectacular than the one from the house. Climbing the steps to the wraparound porch, I took out the second set of keys I'd been given and opened the door. I wasn't expecting much, given the state of disrepair of the main house, so when I opened the door and stepped inside, I was more than pleasantly surprised. The cozy space was dusty, but it looked as if it had been recently renovated and appeared move-in ready. I smiled as I noticed the large stone fireplace on one wall of the main living area. I could imagine how cozy it would be to curl up in front of the fire during a winter storm. The fireplace had a gas insert that looked as if it had been recently installed, but I supposed I should have it checked before I used it. I picked up my phone and added *fireplace guy* to my list.

The living room, which featured hardwood floors and pale gray walls, opened up to a small but newly updated kitchen, which, thankfully, appeared to have working appliances. The space was charming and modern, with granite countertops and updated cabinets. I knew the cottage had two bedrooms, one in the front that looked out over the now-overgrown garden, and one at the back, overlooking the sea.

I poked my head into one of the two bathrooms. The dark gray granite countertops, like those in the kitchen, looked new, which thrilled me, but the cabinets, while updated, had been painted a dark green. Not really my color, but I could always repaint, and the room looked as if it would be adequate once I had the water turned on. Things were definitely looking up, I decided as I headed to the larger of the two bedrooms. The room had a door at the rear that I assumed opened out to a private deck.

"Wow," I said as I took in the view. It was simply amazing.

The dark gray of the winter bay in the distance was bordered by a lush green forest covered with a layer of snow producing an absolutely stunning contrast. The entire shoreline looked to be uninhabited, with the exception of a single dwelling in the distance, perched on the edge of the sea. A feeling of peace rose as the serenity of the landscape wrapped itself around me like a warm hug. I'd always found the sea to have a calming effect on my nerves, even during the worst of times.

Here, I decided, as I took in a deep breath of fresh sea air, was where I'd build my nest. Here in this little guesthouse, where I could both wake up and fall asleep to this spectacular view. I'd need a bed, and possibly a dresser, but for now I'd blow up my air mattress and set it next to the huge glass doors, which I planned to wash as soon as I got my supplies. It would be from this perfect spot, in this little house, that I'd read, dream, refurbish, and heal. I knew the journey to making the main house habitable would be a long one. I knew the road to healing would be even longer. But for the first time since I'd packed my SUV and merged onto Hwy 80 east, I actually believed both might be possible.

Heading back to my SUV, I grabbed my laptop and travel bag. I went back to the cottage, making the first of many trips. Once I had the vehicle unloaded, I sat down at the kitchen counter on one of the stools left behind. I took out my laptop and opened my mail app. I used my phone to take a photo of the fantastic view, then attached it to an email.

I stared at the blank page for several minutes as I worked up the courage to continue. I had done a lot of difficult things in the past year, but for some reason, writing this email seemed harder than most.

Dear Annie,

Greetings from Maine. I've attached a photo of the view from the little cottage where I plan to begin rebuilding my life. Isn't it fabulous? I know you're concerned that I've descended into madness and am no longer in control of my mental faculties, and I understand your trepidation at the choices I've made since the accident, but I needed to do this despite your fears. It would mean so much if you could find it in your heart to understand and support my choice.

Love,
Abby

I read the email through, then let my finger linger over the Send button. Part of me wondered why I bothered, but another part realized that making things right with the only family I had left was a necessary step if I really wanted to rebuild my life.

Chapter 2

Holiday Bay was a charming little town that enjoyed a strong economy centered on the visitors who flocked to the area each year to enjoy the magic of an idyllic seaside community. The downtown section of the tiny hamlet consisted of a single street that featured a variety of shops designed to pull in the visitor with their warmth and charm. Currently, the entire main thoroughfare was in the process of being decorated for the upcoming Christmas Festival, which, according to the signs posted along the narrow country road, would take place weekends and evenings between Thanksgiving and Christmas Eve. I had to admit that, despite my lack of interest in holidays in general since Ben and the baby had died, I found the idea of Victorian carolers, sleigh rides through the snow, and chestnuts roasting on an open fire intriguing.

My first stop after completing a quick survey of the town would be the tiny bakery, which smelled of pumpkin and gingerbread as I passed by. I hadn't eaten since breakfast and I was starving. It was a bit early for dinner, but a sweet treat to tide me over would be just right.

"Can I help you?" asked a plump woman with white hair that matched her white baker's hat and apron. Talk about typecasting. She looked exactly the way you would imagine a fairy-tale bakeshop owner would, right down to the rosy red cheeks and welcoming smile.

"I'll have some of whatever smells so good."

"I've just taken a tray of my famous cinnamon rolls out of the oven. I also have pumpkin pecan muffins and apple strudel that should still be warm."

"A cinnamon roll sounds great. And a cup of coffee. Black."

I sat down at a small round table and waited for my snack to be served. The place was charming, in a Santa's Village sort of way.

"Are you visiting town?" the woman asked as she set a large, gooey cinnamon roll and a mug of steaming hot coffee in front of me.

"I actually live here, as of a few hours ago." I held out my hand. "Abby Sullivan. I bought the house on the bluff."

Her eyes grew large. "You don't say. My name is Mary Cramer, but most folks around here call me Mary Christmas."

I narrowed my gaze. "Mary Christmas?"

She chuckled. "It's a theme name to go along with the spirit of the town."

"Oh, sure." Living in a town where holidays were the main event every single day of the year was going to take some getting used to.

"So you're the brave soul who bought that money pit from Bodine," Mary commented with a chuckle.

I smiled a little half smile. "That's me. Money Pit Abby."

Mary paused. "I'm sorry. It was rude of me to refer to the house as a money pit. It didn't work out for Bodine, but I'm sure you'll make the place grand once again."

"That's the plan, although I'm just going to start with painting two rooms in the cottage. I don't suppose you can point me toward a store where I can buy paint?"

"Buck's place over on Easter Avenue. He can mix you up whatever color you have in mind."

"Thanks. I appreciate the information. The amount of work that needs to be done on the main house is overwhelming, but the cottage is in pretty good shape, so I thought I'd start there."

"Just don't spend all your money on the cottage before you get to the main house, like Bodine did. He was seriously lacking a plan, and that big old place fought him every step of the way."

I plastered on a confident smile. "I'm sure the house and I will get along just fine."

I ate my cinnamon roll and purchased several muffins to take with me, then followed Mary's directions to Easter Avenue. The comment about the house being a money pit had begun to grate on me. Had I just made the biggest mistake of my life? I liked to think I was a logical person who didn't make big mistakes, but I had to admit my tendency to grasp at anything that seemed as if it might help to make my life a bit more tolerable had been my modus operandi during the past year.

The hardware store, like every other store in town, was decorated for the upcoming holiday season. The first thing the customer encountered on walking in from the street was a giant turkey with a sign announcing the daily sales and holiday specials.

"Can I help you, ma'am?" a grizzly man with a thick beard and bright blue eyes asked as I stood in the middle of the doorway, undecided.

"I'm here for paint and painting supplies."

"Aisle seven. I can mix any color you want if you're looking for custom, and I have swatches of some of the more traditional colors if you need inspiration."

"Thanks. I think I'll take a look at your swatches for now. I bought a huge house with a lot of rooms all in need of painting, but I've decided to start with the guesthouse. The rooms I want to paint are green right now, but I'm thinking I'd like to bring the colors of the sea inside. Maybe a rich gray."

"You must be the lady from California who bought the house on the bluff."

"I see word travels fast. I'm Abby Sullivan."

"Buck Owens. The guest cottage was renovated recently and should be move-in ready, but the bluff house hasn't been lived in for more than a generation. It needs a lot of work."

"So I've been told. I understand it's something of a money pit."

Buck chuckled. "I see you've been talking to Mary. She's a wonderful baker, but she lacks vision. Bodine Devine didn't have what it took to recover the majestic lady the house once was, but with the right person to gently nudge the old girl back to life, I know she can be grand once again."

I smiled. "I'm happy to hear that. It will be a big project, but I can see the potential as well."

"Wonderful. I can recommend a good contractor if you're looking for a referral."

"I do plan to hire someone to oversee the project. A referral would be welcome."

"Lonnie Parker," Buck said without hesitation. "He's the best in the area, and he'll treat you fairly. Go on back and start looking at the paint swatches and I'll get you one of his business cards."

"Thanks, Buck. I appreciate it."

By the time I'd visited three additional businesses in search of the basic supplies I thought I'd need to at least get by for a few days, I'd received three more assurances that Lonnie was the best man for the job. If the local chatter was to be taken at face value, he was a hard worker, a hell of a nice guy, and a master craftsman who had a knack for seeing the potential beneath the decay. He sounded too good to be true, but this whole town seemed to be too good to be true, so I decided to take the bull by the horns and call him right away. He informed me that he was just wrapping up a job and would welcome the opportunity to work up a bid for what he assured me would be the grandest home in the county by the time he was finished with it. He estimated he could be out to the house in about an hour, so I took him up on his offer to stop by to take a look around.

******

The days had grown short as winter approached, so by the time the large black truck pulled into the drive, the sun had begun its descent toward the craggy shoreline that formed the western edge of the large bay. Given the fact that the electricity hadn't been turned on in the house yet, I figured a complete tour would most likely need to wait, but I was looking forward to meeting the man I'd heard so much about.

From the main living area, I watched as a large man who looked to be in his midthirties, with sandy blond hair and a pleasant grin, climbed out of the driver's side of the vehicle, then stepped aside as a medium-size dog that looked to my untrained eye to possibly be a Border collie jumped out onto the ground behind him. I walked toward the front door, opened it, and waved to the man who carried a clipboard and a giant flashlight.

"Is it okay if Sadie comes in?" he called out to me.

I assumed he meant the dog and assured him Sadie would be welcome. Maybe he'd even chase away the huge cat I was certain was still lurking somewhere upstairs.

"Lonnie Parker." The man stuck out his hand in greeting.

"Abby Sullivan." I returned the handshake.

"I have to say, you have yourself quite a house here, Ms. Sullivan."

"Abby, please."

"Abby." He nodded. "I've been lusting after this place for years. Would have bought it myself when it came up for sale six years ago if my wife and I hadn't been surprised when our first little bundle of joy turned out to be our first three little bundles of joy."

"You have three children?"

"Six. Three boys, Michael, Matthew, and Mark, who are now six, twin daughters Meghan and Mary, who are three, and a newborn baby girl, Madison."

"Wow. That's really…" I wanted to say *crazy* but settled on "wonderful."

"As you can probably guess, a big job like the one you have here will go a long way toward putting food on the table for all those mouths. If you decide to hire me, I'll do a good job for you."

"Good to know," I answered, somewhat noncommittally. "Should we take a look around? I'm sure if you're familiar with the house, you probably have some idea what needs to be done."

"I do at that. I have to be honest: Turning this rundown gal back into the grand lady I know she can be is going to take not only time but money. I'm not sure what your budget is, but I want you to know we can work together to make the project manageable. I'll write up a bid that will provide a total for the entire project, but I'll also give you subtotals for each portion, so you can pick and choose."

"That would be helpful," I replied.

"Are you planning to turn this into a bed-and-breakfast or an inn?" Lonnie asked.

Was I? I had considered it but hadn't decided yet. I made a living writing fiction, which was a fairly solitary profession, but it had occurred to me that I might make use of the income the house could provide by renting at least a few of the rooms out.

"The thought did run through my mind, but I haven't come to a firm decision. It's a very large house and I'm not sure what I'd do with it if I didn't rent out at least some of the rooms. I've set up a temporary base in the guesthouse, which seems just about perfect for me. An inn might be a good use for the main house, although if I did rent out some rooms,

I'd need to hire someone to run the place. I won't have the time to do it myself."

"The guesthouse was renovated by the former owner, Bodine Devine. He purchased the property about five years ago with the idea of renovating the big house and opening it as an inn, but he only got as far as renovating the cottage for his personal use before his money ran out. He hung on to the place for a while, hoping to find the funding to finish, but he was never able to pull it all together."

"Mary Christmas from the bakery filled me in on Bodine and his ill-conceived plans. It's too bad they didn't work out, but if he hadn't sold, I wouldn't be here, so I suppose I should be grateful."

"If you ask me, he never had the money or the vision to do what he thought he wanted to do. Renovating this house is going to be a huge job, although I have some ideas that might help with the budget. If you want to take a walk-through, we can discuss some options."

"Okay," I said. "Let's take a look."

"The old gal has good bones, so I don't anticipate any structural problems."

"I guess that's a positive. I was curious about the history of the house. I know an English businessman named Chamberlain Westminster had it built in 1895, and Bodine Devine sold it to me just a few weeks ago, but I don't know anything about it in between."

Lonnie paused and turned in a full circle, raising his hands to an empty room, as if somehow revering it. I guess he really was in to the house. "Chamberlain Westminster met a beautiful woman named Abagail Chesterton when he came to this country on business. He fell head over heels in love and wanted to marry her, but she refused to leave her family and move to England, so he built this house and moved here. Four months after they were married, Abagail died from complications relating to pneumonia. Chamberlain was heartbroken. He packed up his things and headed back to England, never to return."

"That's so sad. Should I be weirded out about the fact that the house was built for a woman who had the same first name as me, and that she died four months after moving in?"

"I don't know. Are you weirded out?"

The story was sad, but I didn't feel as if the house was angry about the fate of its first residents, and I didn't have the sense I was going to be haunted by the first Abagail's lingering spirit. "No. I'm not weirded out, but I am intrigued. What happened to the house after Chamberlain went home?"

Lonnie took out a tape and began measuring windows as he spoke. "The house stood empty for almost forty years. Westminster abandoned the house, but he never sold it. He died in a hunting accident in 1932 and his brother, Simon Westminster, inherited it. The brother had no use for a house in the States, so he sold it to a couple from Boston, Jasper and Joslyn Jones. The Joneses fixed the place up and opened a high-end resort. They claimed the saltwater pool they built on the grounds had healing powers, and there were folks who bought into it."

"Did it? Have healing powers?"

Lonnie jotted down some notes on his clipboard, then shrugged. "I doubt it. It was just a pool they had dug. It wasn't like it was a natural spring bubbling up from the ground. I don't suppose it mattered if the pool contained healing water or not. Folks believed it did and they came in droves. The house was a resort and spa until 1954, when the pool was damaged in a hurricane. There was a lot of damage to the entire property, so the resort was closed temporarily and the pool was filled in and covered with lawn. The house was easily repaired, so the resort eventually reopened, but without the pool, it suffered. Eventually, the Joneses gave up and moved away. The house stood empty until Bodine bought it, although there were two other owners between them."

"Who?" I asked, drawn in by the story so far.

"The first was a developer named Clark Ferguson in 1969, with the intention of bulldozing it and building another resort, but his funding fell through. He sold the place to Lester Folkman in 1974, who, like Westminster, planned to renovate it for his bride-to-be. She had other plans and broke the engagement. Lester moved west, and the place was empty until Bodine bought it in 2013."

"It sounds like the house might be cursed. Was anyone ever happy here?"

"From what I know, the Joneses were happy here for a time. They updated the plumbing and electrical to what's here now. I wouldn't worry too much about the history of the place. That's the past, and what you do with the place will become its new reality."

I smiled. "You're right. You know a lot about this place. I can't believe you came up with those names and dates off the top of your head."

Lonnie paused and looked at me. "Like I said, I love this house. I did a lot of research when Folkman decided to sell the place. If not for my growing family, I would have found a way to buy it. Bodine was never a worthy owner for this grand old gal, but the more I talk to you, the more certain I am you're the owner this house has been waiting for."

I had to smile at his poetic turn of phrase, whether it was true or not. "So, let's talk renovation."

Lonnie smiled and nodded.

As we walked through each room, Lonnie provided his vision for the space, but allowed me to respond with my own vision. Some of the rooms only required paint and flooring, while others, such as the kitchen, would need to be gutted and rebuilt from the studs out. There was some electrical and plumbing work necessary to bring it up to code, but he assured me that he could handle everything.

"If you decide to use the house as an inn, you'll want to keep the kitchen sectioned off from the eating and living areas," Lonnie said. "If you don't go that route and this will be your family home, I'd take out this wall and open the whole space up."

Family home. How I wished that was a possibility, but wishing didn't change my bitter reality. "I'm beginning to lean toward the idea of an inn, so for now, we should probably plan on a large commercial kitchen separated from the dining and living areas. If things change, I can always take down the wall later."

"Very true. If you want to open an inn and plan to hire someone to run it, you might want to take out a wall and combine the two downstairs bedrooms into a single space. You could create a suite, with a bathroom and seating area you can use as a live-in option for your inn manager. Ideally, you'll find someone who can both cook and run the place."

"That's a good idea. I'll keep that in mind. Do you know how many rooms I'd have to rent?"

Lonnie jotted down some more notes on the clipboard. "The second and third floor each have a large common area as well as four bedrooms and two bathrooms. You could rework the space so the two bedrooms in each wing on each floor share a central bath, but if it were me, I think I'd reconfigure the space to create four large suites. I know that decreases your available rentals from eight to four, but if each suite featured a large bathroom with a jetted tub, a seating area with a gas fireplace, and a private balcony in addition to a large sleeping area with a view of the sea, I can assure you, you'll get top dollar for them, and it will be less work to have fewer guests."

I raised a brow. "It sounds like you've thought this through."

"I have. When I considered buying the house, it was to open an inn of my own. I was going to call it The Inn at Holiday Bay."

"I like that. Is it okay if I use it?"

"Absolutely."

I slid my hands into the front pockets of my denim jeans as I walked around the large, empty space. "So, the first floor would feature the kitchen, a large dining area for the guests, the main living area, which can be used as a common room, and I assume a guest bath, or at least a half bath, and a suite for the live-in cook and manager."

Lonnie nodded. "In addition, you have that room at the front of the house that I think was initially a parlor. When I was working up my own plans for the house, I was going to use it as a game room. It'd be a perfect place to while away a cold winter's day."

I glanced into the room I'd passed but hadn't explored. "I like that idea as well. The second and third floors would each have two suites, one on either side of the staircase. That would provide my guests with a lot of privacy, which I'm sure would be considered an added bonus."

"Correct. Additionally, each floor has a large room in the center. The one on the second floor has floor-to-ceiling bookshelves, so I assume it was originally used as a library. It has an old stone fireplace you can play with to create a warm, cozy reading area for your guests."

"Sounds wonderful. And the common room on the third floor?"

"It's smaller and empty at this point. You can do whatever you want with it. Maybe an additional seating area? There's a finished attic at the top of the stairs that's packed with boxes and furniture Bodine moved out of the main part of the house when he was preparing to renovate but didn't want to toss in the trash, like he did most of the old furniture that came with the house. It'll take some work to go through all of it, but eventually that space will be usable as well."

"A project for another day."

Lonnie nodded, then looked around. "So, what do you think?"

I smiled. "I like it. Let's go upstairs and take a look."

By the time we completed our walk-through, it had begun to grow dark. Lonnie promised to work up a bid and get it to me in a couple of days. In the meantime, he volunteered to have the gas, electricity, and water turned on the following day, and to have a couple of his subcontractors come by to check everything out at my convenience. Having gas, water, and electricity would make life a whole lot easier, so I happily agreed to provide him with a key and to cover any cost incurred during the start-up.

"Thank you so much for coming by so quickly," I said as we headed back down to the first floor. "I love your ideas. Between us, I think we'll come up with something really special."

"I agree. And I'm very grateful for the opportunity to bid on the project."

I bent down and pet Sadie on the top of the head, which reminded me of my stowaway. "Before you go, there's a cat that seems to have crept in and hidden away somewhere in the house. I don't suppose you'd know how to get rid of him."

Lonnie looked around. "We've been in every room and I haven't seen a cat. Maybe it already left."

"Maybe. I hope so."

"If it shows up again and you need help moving it out, call me and I'll come right over."

"Thank you. I appreciate that. I'm not much of a cat person. In fact, I've never had a pet. Animals sort of freak me out."

Lonnie glanced at Sadie. "I can leave her home next time."

I glanced down at the dog, who was sitting at my feet quietly and politely. "No. Bring her along. Now that I'm living in the country, I need to get used to animals. Sadie here is so sweet. I think she'll be a good dog to start with." I patted her again. "I'll look forward to seeing your bid."

"Should have it in a couple of days."

"Wonderful. I'll walk you out."

After Lonnie left, I made myself a sandwich, poured a glass of wine, and settled into my cozy little cottage to work on some design ideas I'd been playing with since Lonnie started me down the path of choosing colors, materials, and flow patterns. I couldn't remember the last time I was this excited about anything. I looked around my little cottage and decided I definitely wanted to bring the feel of the sea inside, which meant a color pallet of shades of blue, gray, white, and maybe a touch of black for contrast. I closed my eyes and pictured gray walls trimmed in white. Maybe some white wainscoting in a few of the rooms, with black cabinets for contrast. The place was going to be amazing. And the main house…well, it had so much potential, I wasn't sure where to start. I hoped my adequate but finite savings could take the hit. I'd used an inheritance from my grandmother to pay cash for the house and the land it sat on, so at least I didn't have to worry about mortgage payments. I hadn't published anything new since the accident, but the royalties I received from the books I'd written before my world had imploded were enough to get by, and I had the large payout from Ben's life insurance. I'd be fine, I convinced myself, as I wandered over to the window and took in the amazing view of the moon mirroring the water. Simply breathtaking.

It was early still, and I couldn't help but feel antsy. I'd bought a can of medium gray paint I thought I'd use in the master bedroom and bath. I found I had energy to burn, and the walls were in good shape, so they wouldn't need to be sanded and stripped. I headed out to my SUV and grabbed the primer, ladder, and paint brush I'd purchased earlier in the day.

Once I had my supplies, I refilled my wineglass, put on some music, and began rolling on the primer. By the time the walls were ready for paint, I was more than ready for bed, so I decided to finish the next day. I felt content, something I hadn't experienced for a very long time, even though it was the end of a long day that had come at the end of a very long year.

Chapter 3

For a brief moment, before I woke fully, I imagined the weight on my chest to be Ben's arm as he cuddled next to me for a few minutes of intimacy before we went our separate ways. I smiled in my state of drowsiness before I opened my eyes and saw a pair of dark green eyes framed by an orange furry face staring back at me. *Oh God.* I closed my eyes, fighting off the devastation I knew would only cripple me. I should have been prepared for the lingering sorrow, but somehow I wasn't. It was always the worst early in the morning, when a state of half wakefulness allowed me to forget for a brief moment that my entire life had been shattered in the instant it took for a car to swerve into oncoming traffic, killing both Ben and our infant son instantly. It was such a random occurrence, and yet it had forever changed not only my life but that of my husband, who was much too young to die, my son, who had never been given the chance to live, and that of those who knew and loved the funny man I had fallen in love with and married.

"How did you get in here?" I asked the huge cat after opening my eyes once again.

"Meow."

"I see." I looked around the smaller bedroom, where I'd set up my air mattress while I painted the master. "It seems you're quite resourceful, but it's time to get up, which means you have to move."

The cat, who had to weigh at least twenty-five pounds, began to purr but didn't seem inclined to climb off my chest as I'd requested.

"I'm sure you're comfy, and I guess I don't blame you for not wanting to get up given the fact that it's freezing in here, but I have a ton of work to get done today, starting with figuring out where you came from and who you belong to."

The cat nudged his head under my chin as he began to purr even louder.

"It's not going to work. I don't like cats. We're unmixy, like oil and water. Ask anyone."

The cat rolled over onto his back, as if inviting me to give his belly a scratch.

"Sorry, but I don't do belly rubs. Now, move on over so I can climb out of this sleeping bag."

You'd think a sleeping bag tossed over an air mattress would provide a fairly comfortable alternative to a bed, but as it turned out, they didn't quite provide the good night's sleep you'd hope it would. In fact, I felt as if I'd slept on a pile of rocks. Once I managed to free myself from the confines of the sleeping bag, I pushed my fingers into my lower back, pulled on a sweatshirt, then made my way into the bathroom, where I used bottled water to wash my face and brush my teeth. That accomplished, I realized the most important thing I needed to do next was to find coffee. I pulled on a pair of jeans, stuffed my feet into a pair of Nikes, pulled a brush through my hair, and made my way out of the little cottage to my SUV. I glanced back at the cat, who was sitting on the front porch where I'd left him. I felt a twinge of guilt at leaving him behind, but it wasn't like he was a dog and would enjoy a ride in the car. Cats hated cars. Didn't they?

Grumbling under my breath, I climbed out of the SUV and opened the back door. "If you want to come, hop in."

To say I was shocked when the cat trotted across the dirt drive and got into the back seat was putting it mildly. Maybe the creature was some sort of a cat/dog hybrid. It would certainly explain his size.

Thankfully, I didn't have to search too hard for the life-sustaining black liquid that kicked my motor into Drive each morning. The second small business on the left-hand side of the road after pulling onto Christmas Avenue from Halloween Drive was a welcoming coffee shop that advertised "the best biscuits and gravy in town." I pulled over and parked on the street. "You're going to need to wait here. I'm going in to grab some breakfast. I doubt they allow cats. If you're good and don't pee on my floor or shred my seats with those huge claws of yours, I'll bring you something. Do you like sausage?"

"Meow."

"Okay, sausage it is. Now remember, this car needs to be in the same shape it is now when I come back. If it isn't, you won't get the sausage."

The cat jumped onto the front seat, curled into a ball, and settled in for a nap. Maybe he'd behave himself and I hadn't made a huge mistake by bringing him along.

"Have a seat anywhere," the only waitress, a tall woman with gray hair, instructed.

"Do you have a ladies' room?"

"Second door down the hallway at the back of the building."

I headed down the hallway. I was definitely going to need to get my water turned on today, if nothing else. The urge to take a sponge bath was strong, but I settled on washing my hands and splashing water onto my face. I returned to the front and took a seat near the window, where I could keep an eye on my car and the cat I had left inside it.

"Coffee?" asked the woman, whose nametag read *Velma*. I realized the name of the café was Velma's, so she must actually be the owner.

"Please," I answered as I looked around the warm and cozy space, decorated with fall leaves, pumpkins, and corn stalks.

"We have a breakfast special that includes two eggs, hash browns, sausage, and toast for two ninety-nine, or you can order off the menu."

"I'll take the special," I answered. I could save the sausage for the cat.

"Want me to leave a pot?" Velma, who wore a pink uniform that looked like it belonged in the sixties, nodded at the urn of coffee from which she'd poured my mug.

"Please."

She set the urn down. "I'll have your breakfast right out."

Velma called into the kitchen for the special, then went over to the hostess station to answer the phone. I took several long sips of the surprisingly tasty coffee, then took out my phone. If I didn't want to spend another uncomfortable night, I was going to need to accomplish a few things today. Number one was to confirm with Lonnie that he'd been able to get my power and water turned on. I assumed the power and water companies would need to speak to me personally, but Lonnie assured me that he "knew people" and would be able to handle everything with a couple of phone calls. I hoped he was right. Number two on my list was definitely going to be buying a bed. I doubted there was a furniture store in town, but I'd looked it up and it appeared there was a decent-size one less than an hour away. And then there was the cat. The cat I absolutely wasn't going to keep, yet hated to kick out into the cold. If I wasn't able to get him back to his rightful owner right off the bat, I'd need to buy him some food and a litter box.

"Excuse me," I said to Velma as she walked by.

"You need something, sugar?"

I tucked a lock of my unruly brown hair behind my ear. "I recently purchased the old house on the bluff, and when I arrived yesterday, a huge orange cat walked right in and made himself at home. I don't suppose you know who he belongs to?"

"Huge orange cat? About twenty-five pounds?"

I nodded. "That would be him. I'd like to get him back to his owner."

"Can't."

I raised a brow. "I can't? Why not?"

"He's dead. Grange has been gone about a month now. I wondered what happened to Rufus. I'm glad to hear he's okay."

"Rufus is the name of the cat?"

The woman nodded. "I've been worried about him. I'm glad he found someone to watch out for him."

"But I can't keep him," I asserted.

The woman crossed her arms over her ample chest. "Why not?"

Yeah, Abby, why not? "I'm not really much of a cat person. And I've just moved in. I don't even have running water and electricity yet."

"Rufus has been living in the woods for the past month. I don't think he's gonna care about running water or electricity."

I supposed she had a point. "But what about the part about my not being a cat person?"

"Seems Rufus doesn't care much about that either." Velma glanced out at my car. "He with you?"

I nodded.

"Well, bring him in. I'll fix him up something real nice for breakfast. He can eat in the mudroom and you can get him on your way out."

"Are you sure?"

"I never say anything I'm not sure of. Now, run on out and get him. I'll scramble him up some eggs. They're his favorite."

Who would have figured that of all the things I hoped to find in Holiday Bay, a car-riding, egg-eating cat would be the first thing to turn up? Although, technically, I guess he'd found me.

Chapter 4

When we left the diner, Rufus and I headed toward the nearby town, where I hoped the furniture store I'd looked up had a bed in stock and was willing to deliver it, hopefully today. That might be a long shot, especially given the fact that I lived almost an hour away, but it couldn't hurt to ask. I turned the radio to a rock station and turned up the volume. It was a lovely winter day, cold but sunny, and I was enjoying the drive down the coast.

This part of the coastline, with its rugged, rocky appeal, must be lovely in the summer. I could almost picture large sailboats with white sails gliding smoothly over the bright blue water as the sun shone down, creating little sparkles on the surface. One of the things I'd loved most about living in San Francisco was being close to the ocean. Of course, we lived several miles off the actual coast, so the time I'd spent enjoying the beach and the water was significantly less than it was going to be in my new home. I wondered where the nearest beach would be. Maybe I'd ask someone along the way. Winter was just getting underway, so it wasn't as if I was going to make use of a beach right away.

As I neared the town, both small shops and big-lot stores began to appear. I made a mental note of where some of the big-lot stores I'd need when I opened the inn were located. I slowed a bit and looked for the sign for the furniture store I'd been told would announce its presence. I turned on my turn signal and slowed even more as the sign came into view.

I glanced at Rufus as I pulled into a parking spot near the entrance to the warehouse-style store. "You need to wait here. I'm going to see if this store will deliver a bed to the guesthouse. I shouldn't be long."

"Meow." As he had before, the cat curled up and went to sleep. If the cat was going to stay, I'd need a cat bed in addition to a person one. Did furniture stores sell cat beds?

Thankfully, this store was great. Not only did it have a large supply of beds, but it offered same day delivery and was willing to haul whatever I bought all the way out to Holiday Bay for a price. I stretched out on half the beds there before choosing a memory foam mattress I'd been assured would work perfectly with the hardwood bedframe I picked out.

"I'm going to want the matching dresser, wardrobe, and nightstands as well," I said to the salesman who was happily totaling my purchases. "Do you sell cat beds by any chance?"

"Cat beds?"

"Yes. Beds for cats. Do you sell them?"

"No. But there's a pet supply store about a half mile down the road."

"Thanks. These items will do for now." My eyes brushed over a huge dining table that would need to be refinished but would be perfect for the dining area in the main house. "Is this table an antique?"

"It is. I bought it at an estate sale. It'll seat eighteen."

I ran my hand over the dark wood. I didn't need a table that would seat eighteen, at least not yet, but the table was magnificent. "Will it fit in your truck with my bed and other furniture?"

He nodded. "Several of the leaves can be removed. It'll still be a large table, but I'd like to find it a good home, so we'll make it fit."

"Okay, then. I'll take the table as well."

"It doesn't come with chairs."

I shrugged. "That's okay. I can get chairs later."

Rufus was still napping on the front passenger seat when I returned to my SUV. He sat up as I slid into the driver's seat. "We have a bed," I announced. I considered heading down the street to the pet store to find a cat bed, but deep down, I knew that cat would end up in my bed. Of course, I still needed cat food and a litter box, so a trip to the pet store was in the cards anyway. And, as long as I was shopping, I could use some sheets, blankets, and pillows too.

As I drove through town looking for a home goods store, I tried to envision light gray sheets and pillowcases with a dark gray comforter. The gray would look good against the dark wood of the bed. Maybe some throw pillows in varying shades of dark and light blue to add contrast. And an accent piece in black to provide a pop to the setting.

It occurred to me as I wandered up and down the aisles of the home store I found, that I was going to need a lot of furniture and home goods to furnish the big old house I'd just purchased. The renovation was going to be pricy enough; once you added in furniture, bedding, and kitchenware, the total cost to open a commercial property would be astronomical.

Of course, I reminded myself before I freaked myself out completely, once I was able to rent out my four fabulous suites, I'd have income from the inn in addition to what I made with my writing. I had savings to get me started, so as long as I didn't go too crazy, I should be fine.

By the time I'd bought what I needed right away and started back toward Holiday Bay, it was well into the afternoon. I was supposed to meet the delivery truck at four. I was running late and hoped I'd make good time and wasn't thrilled when I found the road closed just half a mile from the side road where I'd turn off to head to the bluff.

"I wonder what happened." I said to Rufus. From the number of flashing red lights, it appeared every emergency vehicle in the area must have responded to whatever was going on. My heart sank when I realized they were turning people around. I hoped there was another road I could take to where I was going. I rolled down my window as a police officer who looked to be barely out of high school walked toward me.

"I'm sorry, ma'am. The road's closed and will be for a while yet. I'm going to need you to turn around."

"What happened?"

"There's been a murder, so local law enforcement has secured this whole area."

The fact that this young cop had just admitted to me that there'd been a murder when he could just as easily have said *incident* or even *accident* surprised me. Ben would have offered a vague reply to a stranger before he had all the facts, but perhaps they did things differently on this side of the country. "I understand you need to close the road, but I'm new here and don't know my way around. I just moved to the house on the bluff. Is there another road I can take there?"

"There's a back road you can take to your place. You'll come in from the south end of the bluff. It'll take you a bit longer and the roads aren't in the best shape, but it'll get you home."

"That'd be great," I said.

"Just do a U-turn here, then take the first right about a half mile back. Head down that road until you come to the second right. After you make that turn, go another five miles or so. I know that seems like a lot; the road loops around and takes you south before you head back north. Eventually, you'll see a big red barn. You can't miss it. Take a left at the barn. The road isn't maintained and will be bumpy, but it'll get you where you're going. Just follow that road until you get to a service road, then stay right at the fork. The fork to the left goes out to the Peyton place, but the right-hand fork will take you right to your place."

"Thank you. I appreciate the directions." I turned the wheel hard to the left to execute the U-turn. "He did say to take the first right?" I asked the cat, suddenly hoping I wouldn't end up lost in the dense forest that claimed most of the land not belonging to the town.

"Meow."

"Yeah, that's what I remember as well. Hang on. It sounds like it's going to get bumpy."

There were a few tense moments along the way as I tried to pick my way along roads that hadn't been plowed by the county yet were passable with four-wheel drive, but eventually, Rufus and I made it home. There was no way the furniture truck was going to make it past the road block. I felt bad they'd come so far and have to turn around, but there wasn't more I could do than call the store to warn them about the situation. The driver had only just left the store, so he turned around, and the delivery was rescheduled for the following day.

Rufus and I had talked about going out for dinner, but I was too rattled to go out again that evening, so we tried out the water and electricity, which had been turned on thanks to Lonnie and his connections. I made a sandwich and Rufus had a bowl of the food the woman at the pet store had assured me he would enjoy once he got used to it.

I ate, then called Lonnie. "Thank you so much. You have no idea how happy I was to come home to water and electricity."

"Not a problem. Like I said, I know people. I came by when you were out and ran the water so the pipes would flush. I wanted to make sure you didn't have any leaks, which you don't. As it turned out, the main waterline had been turned off at the source, so I turned that on for you too."

"Thanks again. You have no idea how grateful I am."

"Just part of the full-service experience I offer my customers. I couldn't get the gas turned on until someone from the gas company came out and did an inspection, so you don't have the use of the stove or heater yet."

"That's fine. Once the gas is turned on, I'd love to use the fireplace in the cottage. Can we get someone out to inspect that?"

"We can. It's gas and fairly new, so you should be good to go once the gas company comes by. The woodburning fireplaces in the main house might be an entirely different story, though. I'll have someone out tomorrow to look at all the fireplaces. If you decide to rent the upstairs rooms in the main house, you'll want to convert to gas. It's cleaner, and you won't have to worry about carrying wood up the stairs."

I walked over to the window and looked out at the sea as I answered. "That's a good point. Include the conversion in your bid."

"I'm including everything, so you can pick and choose. Even the exterior of the place and the yard."

I flinched. "I hadn't even considered the yard." As I looked around at the land revealed from where I stood, I knew it was going to be expensive.

"Like the house, it's going to need a lot of work. You'll want an outdoor seating area at the back of the house where it overlooks the sea. You might even consider serving meals out there in the summer. And of course you'll want to have a nice presentation at the front of the property; that's the first thing your guests will see."

"Sounds expensive."

"It could be, but I know some folks. I can barter on your behalf for some of the labor and get you a discount on the materials. Once the snow melts, we'll draw up a plan. The exterior of the house is going to be as amazing as the interior. In fact, if you want, I can ask a buddy of mine who owns a nursery down the coast to come up to talk to you about the shrubs and trees you might want to consider. You won't want to plant until the spring, but it's never too early to start planning."

"I'd appreciate that. I knew this would be a huge job when I bought the place, but suddenly I'm feeling a bit overwhelmed."

"You'll have a real showplace when we're done. How did the shopping go?"

I filled Lonnie in on my purchases, and that the furniture wouldn't be delivered until tomorrow because of the road closure. I asked if he knew of anyone who refinished furniture, and as it happened, his wife, Lacy, did it on the side. He'd built her a complete woodshop on their property so she could work when the kids were napping. He suggested I give her a call when I'd taken delivery of the table.

Later, Rufus and I headed into the bedroom. After priming the walls the previous evening, I was feeling motivated to paint. Before I began, however, I had another telephone call I needed to make. A call I'd been putting off but was a necessary part of my healing. Before Ben and baby Johnathan died, I'd worked long hours on my writing, but my writing had been on the back burner so I'd have plenty of time for laying around and wallowing in self-pity. Not that self-pity hadn't been justified, but I'd realized at last that it wasn't helpful or healthy.

I'd been thinking about finally contacting my agent about the book that was almost a year late and knew in my gut now was the time to do it. I picked up my phone and scrolled through for my agent's cell number.

"Kate. It's Abby."

"Abby? Abby Sullivan?"

"Yes, it's me, Abby Sullivan. I know it's been a while since we've spoken, but I think I'm finally ready to reenter the land of the living." My announcement was met with silence. "Kate? Are you there?"

"I'm here. I'm just so happy to hear from you. How have you been? Wait, don't answer that. I know how you've been. I'm sorry I'm babbling, but I'm not sure what to say."

"That's okay. I'm used to people not knowing what to say."

Kate's voice softened. "Yeah, I bet you are. I've really missed you. And I think of you often. I keep meaning to call, but then I have no idea where to start, so I end up putting it off." Kate paused. "I'm sorry. I bet everyone has been treating you that way, and I bet that makes things worse."

Now that was an understatement. "It's okay. It can be awkward to know how to deal with someone else's tragedy, and to be honest, until the moment I arrived in Maine, I wasn't sure I wanted to talk to anyone anyway."

"Maine?"

"I bought a house in a small town called Holiday Bay."

"I thought you liked the city."

"I did. Now I don't. I needed a change."

"Yes." Kate paused. "I can understand that. I know this is going to be the dumbest question ever asked, but how are you really doing?"

"Honestly?" I took a deep breath. "I have good days, like today, when I feel determined to rebuild my life. But there are other days when the reality of my loss cripples me, and I wonder if I'll ever be able to function again. Making the decision to start over was hard, but it was something I needed to do. A change of scenery should help with the process. At least I hope it will."

"If there's anything I can do, you just need to shout."

"I know you're there for me. And I appreciate it. For now, what I need most is to get back to work. Do you think my publisher has totally written me off?"

Kate hesitated. "Totally, no. But that doesn't mean we won't need to wow them to get back on their schedule. Are you thinking of finishing the manuscript you were working on before the accident?"

"No. I don't think I have the heart to finish that particular book. I'm thinking of spending the next week or two coming up with something new. I'd been kicking around an idea for a psychological thriller even before the accident. I'm sure I can come up with something that will knock everyone's socks off."

"I'm excited to see what you come up with. Why don't you get a couple of sample chapters down on paper and send them to me? We can chat again then."

I smiled as a spark of creative energy I hadn't felt for a very long time pushed its way through my grief. "I will. And if you have time, you should plan a trip to my neck of the woods. I bought a huge old house I'd love to show you. It needs a lot of work, but it's mine."

"What are you going to do with a huge old house?"

"Open an inn, actually."

"An inn?"

"I know it's crazy, but I finally realized it was going to take a little crazy for me to nudge myself out of the mire of hopelessness and grief I'd settled into."

"I guess that makes sense. And I've always wanted to take a drive up the coast. Do you have snow?"

"We do. Not a lot yet, but enough to provide atmosphere."

"Wow." Kate paused. "Abby Sullivan living in Maine. In a small town no less. I'm still trying to wrap my head around that. Do you think you'll be happy?"

Did I? Maybe not totally. At least not for a while. But I was better, and better could be its own kind of happy. "Yes. I think I'll be happy. Or at least on my way there."

Kate and I spoke for a few more minutes. It felt good to talk to someone from my past without breaking into tears. Most of the time I tried not to think about Ben and Johnathan and the distracted driver who'd swerved into their lane and ripped them from my life. It was too painful to remember what we'd had, too overwhelming to consider what we'd planned for our lives.

I changed into old clothes and began rolling the first layer of paint onto the bedroom walls. The sky had grown dark, but thanks to Lonnie, tonight I had an overhead light to brighten the room. While the paint was drying, I laid out the crown molding and began painting it white. There was something about freshly painted walls that made things feel new and somehow untainted. I'd decided to paint the walls in the bathroom the same color as the bedroom. Once the cottage was whipped into shape, I'd turn my attention to the book I was beginning to develop in my mind.

As my mind worked through various scenarios, the memory of the emergency vehicles on the road flashed into my mind. The officer had said there'd been a murder. I wondered who'd died and who they'd left behind. I now knew that the loss of a loved one was the single hardest thing a person would ever have to endure. I said a little prayer for the family I imagined was grieving just as I had a year ago. I hoped the person responsible for the senseless death was swiftly brought to justice, unlike the one who'd caused Ben to swerve to avoid hitting him head-on and then driven away before the emergency vehicles had responded. There wasn't a day that went by that I didn't find myself wishing the coward who'd left a man and baby to die would ultimately get the punishment he deserved.

Chapter 5

I woke to snow flurries the next morning. I hoped the storm didn't intensify to the point where the truck from the furniture store wasn't able to make the trip. I had a kink in my neck I wasn't sure I'd ever work out after just two nights on the floor. I hadn't ended up with much for dinner the night before, so I decided to take Rufus and head to town for a hot breakfast. I knew Velma would welcome Rufus, so although there were several diners that served breakfast, I returned to the same one from the day before.

"Good morning, Velma," I said as I walked in with Rufus trailing along behind me.

"Coffee?"

"Please." I hung my cherry red parka on the rack near the front door.

"Today's special is sausage gravy over homemade biscuits with scrambled eggs on the side."

"Sounds good. And scramble up a couple of eggs for Rufus as well."

Velma smiled. "I'm glad to see he's still with you."

I glanced down at the cat. "No one could be more surprised than I am. I'm definitely not a cat person, but this particular one is beginning to grow on me. Although," I added, "he's a bit of a bed hog."

"You still sleeping on that air mattress?"

I nodded. "Unfortunately, with the road closure yesterday, the truck with my bedroom furniture was unable to make it to my place. I'm hoping it'll be able to make the trip today. I bought a king, so there should be plenty of room for both Rufus and me."

Velma looked out the window. "I don't think we're supposed to get much snow."

"Did you hear what happened yesterday?" I asked as the song on the radio changed from a popular country song to a Christmas classic. 'Twas the season for the spirit of the holiday to begin to seep into everyday life. "All the officer I spoke to told me was that there was a murder."

"Unfortunately, a local girl was found dead in the woods. Darcy Jared. She was only twenty-two. Worked as a waitress at the Reindeer Roundup."

"Oh no. I'm so sorry. What happened?"

Velma sighed. I could see the death of this young woman had affected her deeply. "No one knows. She was last seen leaving the bar after her shift on Saturday night. I spoke to Colt Wilder yesterday. According to one witness, Darcy was last seen with her boyfriend, Adam Lagerfeld. I'm not sure if the police have had a chance to interview him, but Colt will be in later, so I'll ask him then."

"Colt Wilder?"

"Oh, sorry, that's Chief Wilder."

"Do you see Chief Wilder every day?"

Velma nodded. "He's single and doesn't like to cook, so he has breakfast with me every morning and dinner with Gilda down the street every evening."

"It's nice there are warm, friendly places to have a meal."

"Folks around here enjoy getting together to share a meal and catch up on the local news. Normally, it's a lot busier in here in the morning, but November's a slow month. We do a steady business in the summer, and then we have the crowd that comes north for the leaf tour in the fall, but once the trees are bare, things slow down until after Thanksgiving. You're lucky to have arrived before the Christmas crowd. It can get plumb crazy once the festival starts."

"Does it run every day between Thanksgiving and Christmas?"

"To an extent. Weekends are the busiest, but there are folks who come out for the lights and window displays pretty much every day of the week."

"Sounds festive."

Velma topped off my coffee. "It's something special. Once you open your inn, you'll want to get involved. The whole town commits. That's one of the reasons the festival is so popular."

I raised a brow. "How did you know I was thinking about opening an inn? I'm pretty sure I didn't mention it yesterday."

Velma shrugged. "Word gets around."

"I see." The fact that what I considered to be personal news had already made the rounds was a bit disconcerting, but I guess I'd need to get used to small-town gossip. "From the street names and the name of the town, I'll assume Christmas isn't the only holiday you do up big."

"You'd be right about that. This town was built on its reputation for celebrating seasons and holidays in a big way. We have a harvest festival in the fall, the Christmas Festival in the winter, and an Easter Parade and egg hunt in the spring. Then there are Fourth of July celebrations, lobster festivals, clam bakes, and local festivals like Founders Day. You can't find a month on the calendar when you won't trip over folks celebrating one event or another."

"I suppose that could be fun."

Velma nodded. "It's a lot of work to organize all those events, but this is a small town, and the funding for local programs is sparse. We do what we can with what we get from the state, but most of our budget is made up with what we can raise from the tourists who pass through."

"I'll need a few months to get settled, but I'm sure I'll find ways to help out where I can."

"We have an event committee meeting every week. I'll get you the information when you're ready. Even if you won't have time to volunteer right away, attending the meetings is a good way to meet the folks who'll be your neighbors."

"The committee sounds like a wonderful way to dip a toe in the community pool."

Velma looked toward the counter. "Your order is up. Do you want fruit on the side?"

"No. The eggs and biscuits and gravy will be fine."

I settled in with my food, enjoying the winter wonderland outside the window. I had never lived where it snowed before, and I looked forward to it. I needed to call Lonnie today to see if he had managed to get hold of the fireplace guy to turn mine on. It would be nice to curl up next to a fire with a glass of wine and a good book while it snowed outside. Yes, I thought as I watched people in brightly colored parkas hurry by the window, making their way to work or wherever they needed to be, I was going to like it here just fine.

******

After breakfast I went back to the cottage to finish painting the bedroom in anticipation of the arrival of the furniture. I'd called the furniture store to confirm that they still planned to deliver it, and they assured me the truck would arrive no later than one o'clock that afternoon.

The paint on the walls had dried, as had the crown molding and baseboard. All I needed to do was to hang it. When the furniture arrived, the bedroom would be done. The cabinets in the bathroom wouldn't take long to paint. Maybe I'd tackle them next.

As I hammered and sawed, I thought about the girl whose body had been found in the forest. The fact that she was both young and a local was going to hit the community hard. I hadn't had a chance to meet Chief Wilder, but Velma said he was an intelligent and capable man, so I hoped he'd be able to find the killer sooner rather than later. When Ben had a tough case, he'd often explain the basic elements to me and then we'd throw what-ifs around until we hit upon something that made sense. I wasn't a cop and didn't have the training he did, but he'd often told me I had a natural knack for hitting on just the detail others had missed. I wouldn't go so far as to say he needed me to do his job, but he appreciated the insight I provided.

God, I missed him.

I'd lost others in my life, but losing my husband was so much worse than anything I'd previously experienced. When my parents died I was sad, and I still missed them, but I'd had my dreams to hang on to. When Ben died, all my dreams and the plans we'd made had died with him.

I fought back a tear and returned my focus to the room around me. Allowing myself to sink back into depression wasn't going to bring Ben back, nor was it going to help me move on with my life. I glanced out the window at the gray sea. An amazing view, even without the sun in the sky.

I was just finishing up the baseboard when I noticed what looked like a shadow pass the window at the back of the big house. I was sure there wasn't anyone there, and I remembered locking it up tight, so the shadow was probably a trick of the light caused by a passing cloud. Still, I wanted to be sure, so I grabbed my keys and went over to check. I entered the house through the back door and took a look around, but nothing seemed to have been disturbed. I checked the front door too, and all the ground-floor windows, which were all locked. I headed upstairs, although there was no way anyone could get in through those windows unless they were Spider-Man.

I peeked into the first bedroom, which appeared to be empty. Most of the rooms were covered with a thick layer of dust, including the floor of the one where I was standing. There were no footprints, other than the ones near the door, which Lonnie and I had made, so I closed the door and continued to the second bedroom. It too was empty. I searched each room until I ended up in the large one with the shelves, which we'd talked about using as a library and reading room. There were footprints on the floor well inside, but this was a room Lonnie and I had entered and inspected in much more detail than the empty bedrooms. I didn't notice anything out of place, but I had the oddest feeling I was missing something.

I headed back downstairs and into the kitchen. I looked around once again, but as before, nothing appeared to have been disturbed. On a whim, I opened the door to the basement and peered into the darkness. I felt along the wall for a switch. After a minute of searching, I found what I was looking for. Overhead lights revealed a large unfinished space.

The basement was empty except for an old mattress that had been tossed onto the cement floor and several boxes, which I imagined an owner had forgotten to take when they moved, were lined up against a far wall. I went down the rest of the steps, crossed the room, and opened the lid of the first box, revealing a letterman's sweater, a set of pom-poms, and a book. I found a ring tucked under the book, and an envelope full of photos beneath that, all of a young girl who looked to be in her late teens with blond hair and green eyes.

I closed the box and opened the next one over. It too contained random items: a Holiday Bay High School T-shirt, a silver bracelet, worn running shoes, and another envelope, this one filled with photos of a girl with dark hair and brown eyes. Each of the four boxes contained similar items, probably the possessions of a teenage girl. Maybe I'd ask the Realtor if he knew who they might belong to.

It was almost time for the furniture truck to arrive and I didn't want to risk missing it, so I closed the lids on all the boxes and climbed back up the stairs, turned off the light, and went back to the guesthouse.

Chapter 6

Lacy Parker was adorable. Despite having carried and delivered six children in six years, she was petite and energetic. I'd called her about refinishing the dining table. If she was interested in taking on the work and had space to store it, it might make sense to have the truck driver make a side trip to her place after he delivered my bedroom set. She was thrilled to take on the project and the driver was willing to make the extra stop, so after he set up my bed and arranged the other furniture, I followed him to the address Lacy had given me.

"I love this table," Lacy trilled, her long dark curls bouncing up and down as she hugged her arms to her chest.

"It needs a lot of work," I said with a tone of caution.

Lacy ran her hands over the surface. "It does show signs of age. It has to be a hundred years old or more. But the lifelines that run through the wood only make it more interesting."

"Lifelines?"

"Most people just call them scratches, but each scratch has a story." Lacy ran a finger over a deep gash as if it were her lover. "People, real people, with joys and sorrows and dreams and challenges, have sat at this table and shared those emotions with the people they dined with. Where most people see a mar on the surface of the wood, I see a young mother having a meal with her children, or a couple making plans for their future. I see grandmothers rolling out cookie dough while their grandchildren look on, and teenagers doing homework while their father makes his way home from a busy day at work. I see births and deaths and weddings and life."

"Wow." I put a hand to my chest. "That's beautiful."

"Of course, the stories are the table's to keep, but I like to daydream as I bring new life to an old piece."

I laughed. "You sound like Lonnie when he talks about the house."

She smiled. "I guess that's what makes us so good together. We both value the past as we look forward to the future. If you stop to consider how many people have most likely dined at this table in the past century, it could blow you away. Historical pieces like this one aren't easy to find. Where did you get it?"

I gave her the name of the furniture store.

"I haven't been there. I'll have to stop by when I have the time." Lacy ran her fingertips lovingly along the wood again. "We'll need to settle on a finish. I have samples so you can get an idea of how it will look with different stains. And we'll need to look for chairs that couple nicely with it. I know a few places where we might be able to get the perfect thing."

Lacy's blue eyes shone with excitement as she got down on the floor and took a closer look. "I can't wait to get started. Thank you so much for thinking of me."

"Your husband said you were the best."

"He's biased, but I *am* the best, and I'll make your table beautiful."

"I know you will. And there's no hurry. The table is for the inn and I'm a long way from needing it. Is Lonnie out on a job today? I wanted to talk to him about the house."

"He's finishing up something, but I know he planned to call you about stopping by later. He's been working on your bid almost nonstop since you first spoke. I've never seen him so excited about a job. He was practically drooling while he was looking through his flooring samples."

I couldn't help but smile. The enthusiasm of the couple was infectious. "I'm heading into town for a few supplies and home after that, so if you speak to him, tell him to come on by."

"I'll do that. Lonnie said you're a writer."

I raised a brow. "I am. I'm surprised he knows that, though."

"He likes to do his homework. It's important to him to know who he's working with, so if he doesn't know a potential client, he usually asks around. I wish I could say I have a lot of time to read, but with six children and a part-time business, I really don't. I pick up a book at the library every now and then; I'll have to look for something you've written the next time I'm there. Do you write romance?"

I nodded. "I have a few romance novels on the shelf, as well as some women's fiction from my early days, but in the last few years I've switched to mysteries and thrillers. I'm thinking about writing a psychological thriller for my next novel."

Lacy made a face. "I'm not sure I'd like the suspenseful, gory stuff. I'm afraid my imagination is too active to prevent the images of serial killers and brutal murders to spill over into my dreams. I can't watch movies like that either. But if you have any romances, I'll definitely try one. Something sweet and heartfelt without a lot of graphic sex would be perfect."

"I have a book that would suit you perfectly. No need to buy it or even borrow it from the library. I'll have my agent send you a copy. I usually keep some books on hand, but when I made the trip east I only brought what I could fit in my SUV. I plan to have my stuff shipped once I get settled."

Lacy looked at the baby monitor in her hand, turned slightly, and headed toward the door of her little workshop. I followed. "Lonnie said you've settled into the cottage."

"I have." I followed Lacy out into the snow. "And it's been wonderful."

"The view is to die for," Lacy said as we crossed the yard. "I could totally imagine waking up to that every morning. Although you're pretty isolated out there. Does it make you nervous to be all by yourself with a possible killer on the loose?"

"I'm not the sort to spook easily, and I have a killer cat to protect me." I smiled. "But the idea that whoever killed that young woman might still be out there has given me a few uncomfortable moments. Have you heard anything?"

"Not a lot. There's gossip going around, so it's hard to separate fact from fiction. I did hear Colt is going to talk to both her boyfriend, Adam Lagerfeld, and her best friend, Carly Smith. I imagine he's hoping Darcy told someone where she was heading when she left the bar. Initially, I'd heard she was with Adam, but then I heard a rumor about Adam that turned out to be wrong and she was last seen alone that night. Colt will sort it all out."

"Colt is the chief of police?"

"Yes. I'm sorry, I should have said. He's Lonnie's best friend, so to us he's just Colt. He's a good guy and a good cop. I'm sure he'll do whatever he needs to do to put the snake who killed Darcy behind bars." Lacy paused. "Sounds like Madison is up from her nap. Walk upstairs with me and we can continue to chat while I change her."

I wasn't sure being around a six-month-old baby was a good idea. Not that I didn't like babies, but ever since I lost Johnathan, I'd found myself getting choked up at the mere sight or scent of a baby. I wanted to think my heart was healing and I'd soon be whole again, but then I wondered if that were really true, if it ever would be.

"How are you, princess?" Lacy said after opening the door to a cute pink-and-white bedroom containing more stuffed animals than any kid would ever need.

A dark-haired cutie with curly hair and blue eyes broke into a grin when her mother walked into the room. Lacy lifted her out of the crib, then cradled her close to her chest. She kissed the red-cheeked baby on the top of the head and carried her to a changing table. "This is Abby," Lacy said to the baby as she put her down.

The baby didn't seem overly impressed with me. In fact, she was a lot more interested in the stuffed panda her mother had given her to hold while she changed her diaper.

"It looks like you need dry clothes as well," Lacy said to the adorable child. She stripped off her damp clothing, then picked her up wearing only the diaper. Lacy looked at me. "I have clean clothes in the dryer."

I nodded and followed her down the stairs. When we arrived in the laundry room, Lacy held the baby out to me. "Can you hold her for a minute while I sift through the dryer for her Tom the Turkey jumper?"

I took a step back, as if Lacy had been trying to hand me a rattlesnake.

Lacy pulled the baby toward her chest. "Is everything okay?"

Not really. I didn't want to launch into a long conversation about it, though, so I tried to smile and take a step forward. "I'm fine. I just…"

Lacy's eyes grew soft. "Of course. Lonnie told me. I'm so sorry. I wasn't thinking."

I blew out a breath. "It's okay." I looked at the chubby baby in Lacy's arms. "I just haven't held a baby since…"

Lacy grabbed the first jumper she came across and slipped it onto the baby. "I really am sorry. I don't know what to say."

I forced a smile. "No apology necessary. I guess I'm not quite as ready as I thought to be integrated into some aspects of life. I should be past this by now. It's been a year."

Lacy walked into the connected kitchen and put the baby in the high chair. "Grief takes as long as it takes. Don't let anyone tell you differently. If you aren't ready to hold a baby, you should wait until you are."

I looked toward the ceiling, a move I had learned would sometimes help to quell my tears. "Thank you for understanding. Not everyone does."

Lacy looked at me with such pity in her eyes that I wanted to scream. I made small talk for a while longer before Lacy said she had to pick up the older kids from school. The ease with which she got the younger three ready and then strapped them into the car seats in her van was truly amazing. Johnathan had only been five weeks old when he'd died. I hadn't had a chance to get into a groove as a new mother, though I'd been exhausted most of the time. And I only had one baby. I couldn't imagine how difficult it must have been during those first few weeks of parenthood with triplets to care for.

I'd loved Johnathan with all my heart, but being a mother hadn't ever been part of our plan. Ben was busy climbing through the ranks of the San Francisco Police Department. He'd recently made detective and was gunning for captain. I had my writing career, which was going well. Not only had I recently made the *New York Times* Best Sellers list, but I'd secured a multibook contract with a very nice advance.

Life had been good. Life had been hectic. Children had been the farthest thing from our minds until my doctor informed me that the flu that simply wouldn't go away wasn't a flu at all but a baby. Initially, we'd been shocked. We were both so busy, we barely had time to commit to our marriage let alone a baby. But after the initial surprise had worn off, we'd warmed to the idea. By the time Johnathan was born, we were so in love with this tiny little person that all our doubts vanished.

After Johnathan, life had felt complete. Until…

Chapter 7

Deciding not to think about the *until*, I turned on the radio and drove to the market. As I turned onto Halloween Drive, I passed a small building with red and green flashing lights that announced to anyone passing by that the Reindeer Roundup had half-price pints until six o'clock. On a whim, I pulled into the mostly empty parking lot. I couldn't explain the urge to check out the place where Darcy Jared was last seen alive. I supposed I just needed a diversion from my reignited emotions. That was the only thing that made sense, because I'd never met her, and her murder didn't have anything to do with me. But my heart was screaming in despair and I wanted it to stop. Being both a mystery writer and a homicide detective's widow, I'd developed a curiosity that had me wondering about the rest of the story, and that, in this case, was just the diversion to pull myself out of my current unhappiness.

I entered the dark building, sauntered over to the bar, and took a seat.

"Can I help you?" asked a man I estimated to be in his late forties.

"I'll have a pint of whatever you have on special."

"I have a nice Christmas lager."

"Sounds fine." I looked around while the bartender poured my drink. The lack of windows should have made the space depressing, but the fireplace on one wall, the shiny hardwood floors, the rich pine tables scattered around the pine-paneled bar, and the comfy booths along one wall gave it a cozy feel.

"Are you here on vacation?" he asked after setting my ale in front of me.

"I just moved here. I bought the big house on the bluff. My name is Abby Sullivan."

"Denver Thomas," he replied. "I heard someone bought the bluff house. You've taken on quite the project."

I wished people would stop saying that. It was causing all sorts of angst I wasn't prepared to deal with. I made a noncommittal reply, then asked about the girl whose body had been found in the woods.

"Darcy Jared."

I nodded as I took another sip of the beer. "I understand she left here on foot the night she disappeared. This town seems like the sort of place one could walk around at night and not be in danger. I'm sorry to find out that isn't the case."

"I don't think the town or its residents are the problem," Denver replied as he began to wipe the already spotless bar. "Darcy was a friendly girl. Overly friendly, in my opinion. Her habit of striking up conversations with the customers from out of the area was the main reason she received such big tips, but I warned her more than once that being too familiar with folks she didn't know had the potential to get her into trouble."

"So you think she was killed by someone who was passing through?"

He picked up a different rag and began drying glasses. "Had to have been. There isn't anyone around here who would do such a thing."

"I don't suppose you have a theory as to who might have killed her?"

He looked at me with suspicion on his face. "You some kind of a cop?"

"Mystery writer."

"Oh, sure," he said, although he continued to look cool. "Guess being the curious sort is part of the job."

"Yes, I guess it is." I slipped a twenty out of my purse and set it on the bar.

He glanced down at it, then began to speak again. "I can't say who might have killed Darcy. At least not for sure. There was a group in the bar that night from somewhere way south. I think I heard South Carolina. They were on their way to a hunting lodge north of here to do some kind of male bonding thing. Planned to be there for several weeks. Anyway, they drank a lot, and with an overabundance of alcohol comes a lowering of inhibitions. The drunker they got, the more money they tossed around. Darcy was all over it. Flirting and whatnot. One of the guys got a little handsy, but she handled it. Still, I noticed that when she rejected him, he gave her a look."

I raised a brow. "What kind of look?"

"You know. The kind that promises that while he might be willing to take a break, things weren't over between them just yet."

"You were working that night?"

"No. I work days. I was here with a couple of friends. We have a pretty heated darts tournament going on."

I turned to the back wall, where several dartboards were hung. "I don't suppose you caught the name of the guy who gave Darcy the look?"

"Nope. And if I did know it, I wouldn't say. At least not to you. A little girl like you ought not to get involved in tracking down a coldblooded killer, no matter how curious you are," he scolded. "This town survives on its reputation as a warm, cozy small town with buildings made of gingerbread and roads made of cotton candy. Finding another little girl dead in the woods wouldn't be good for business at all, now would it?"

I wanted to assure him that I could handle myself but rolled my eyes instead. He was a chauvinist who would never understand it didn't take testosterone to be self-sufficient. I found I wasn't in the mood for a beer after all and left the twenty on the bar, got up, and went back to my car.

I'd just gotten back at the cottage when Lonnie called to let me know he could be by in an hour if that was convenient. I made a quick sandwich while I waited for him. I had to admit I was a little nervous. After talking to Lonnie about the possibilities the house had to offer, I'd become really excited about tackling everything right away. I just hoped I could afford to do that. I didn't know a lot about home remodel and repair, but it seemed as if renovating a couple of rooms could eat up most of my budget.

I expected Lonnie and Sadie to show up with a document several pages in length given the scope of the project; what I didn't expect was for him to have not only a very detailed bid but a binder with photos, drawings, material and color samples, and even a section on redoing the outdoor space come spring.

"Wow," I said. "You're really are thorough."

"This is a major renovation. You'll have a lot of choices to make. Not only in terms of finances and priorities, but also colors, materials, overall concept. I wanted you to have everything you needed to help bring your vision to life."

I'd never been involved in a remodel before, large or small, but from the work he'd already done, I could see why he'd been so highly recommended when I'd asked around town. "This is great. So great. I don't even know where to start."

"You might want to start with the budget, although I think you should be sitting down when you do. Don't let the total freak you out. You don't have to do everything I've priced out, and even for the things you decide to go ahead with, you don't have to do everything at once."

I opened the binder and found the tab labeled *budget*. Hello six figures. Not that I was surprised by the amount exactly, but it was sobering to see it written down in black ink.

"If you look here," Lonnie pointed to additional tabs, "I have things broken down several different ways. If you want to know how much it would cost to do just the floors, you can look at the flooring tab, which takes into consideration several options from refinishing to replacing. If you prefer to tackle things by room, I have budgets worked out for each room, depending on which materials you choose. I know the cost as a whole is overwhelming, but if you break it down, I hope you'll find it manageable."

I took a deep breath and blew it out slowly. I looked at the total again, then leafed through each page. Lonnie had done a thorough job. I felt a mild panic attack coming on but fought it down. I knew what I wanted and I knew how to get it. At least I thought I did. I took another breath and then looked up at Lonnie. "Okay."

"Okay to which part?"

"All of it," I said with more conviction than I felt. "I bought this house with the intention of refurbishing it, so let's refurbish it."

"You did notice the cost at the bottom of the page?"

I nodded. "It's a lot of money, I admit, but I'm looking forward to the project. I know it's going to cost a lot, and it might make sense to do the renovations spread out over time, but I can't continue to do construction after I begin renting out the rooms, so I think we should go for it and get it all done up front. What I'd like to do now is come up with a plan so I can work out a budget and a timeline."

Lonnie hugged me hard enough to chase the breath from my chest. "Thank you. I can't begin to tell you how much this means to me."

I hugged him back, trying to catch some air as I did so. "It means a lot to me as well. You really have no idea. When can we start?"

"How about Monday? I'll need to get materials ordered, but there's a lot of teardown to see to, and we can start that right away."

"Monday works for me. I think I'd like to start with the kitchen. It's the most expensive part, so I'd like to get it out of the way."

"Sounds workable."

"I've been fooling around with some sketches I feel will make the most of the space. My number-one priority is windows. A lot of them. I want to be able to see all the way down the coast. I'm also going to want to convert the fireplaces to gas, as we talked about. I'll leave the pacing of the renovations to you once we get started. How long do you think it will take to complete? I'd love to be able to begin renting rooms by this summer."

Lonnie paused before he answered. I liked the fact that he was really thinking about my question, not just spouting off the answer he thought I was looking for. "We can certainly shoot for late June or early July. I'm going to start lining up subcontractors right away. As long as we don't run into any unforeseen problems, we should be able to get the place finished by the time the tourist season really kicks in. I'd like to walk through the house again to make some decisions that will help me line up materials and subcontractors."

We agreed the kitchen would be a total gut job. It would be fun to start from scratch, but I'd need to pick out cabinets, countertops, flooring, and appliances. I also wanted to convert one of the half baths on the first floor into a walk-in pantry. It was an awkward room anyway and would provide a lot of additional storage. In terms of aesthetic appeal, the most important thing would be to remove the small slider off the kitchen and put in a bank of French doors that would bring in a lot of natural light.

I wanted a lighter feel overall in the kitchen and eating area, so we talked about sanding down the dark floors and refinishing them in a lighter shade. The cabinets would be dark, the granite for the countertops light, and the walls painted a neutral color to tie everything together. I was a little disappointed we couldn't remove the wall separating the kitchen from the dining area to create an open concept, but once I started having guests, a division between work and eating space would be preferable. Once the glass doors were added, the space was going to be bright and cheery even without the open concept.

As for the upstairs, I definitely wanted to go with the four suites. It made sense to offer fewer luxury units rather than more with shared baths. Each suite would have sleeping and sitting areas with a gas fireplace, as well as a private balcony and jetted tub. I loved the idea of a library for the common room on the second floor and a seating area for the smaller common room on the third floor. I'd been calling the room on the first floor near the entry the game room in my mind, so I referred to the one on the third floor as the parlor. For some reason, I felt it important that each room have its own name. I even planned to name the suites once I'd given it some thought.

After we'd gone through the entire house, I walked Lonnie out to his truck. He paused and looked at me. "I have something to say I'm not sure I should."

"It's okay. What is it?"

"Lacy called me after you left today. She told me what happened. With the baby. She felt terrible and wanted me to make sure you understood how very sorry she was."

I placed my hand on Lonnie's arm. "I know. She didn't do anything wrong and it wasn't her fault. Most of the time I'm fine, but every now and then, everything comes rushing back." I took a moment to gather my thoughts. "I like Lacy. I want us to be friends and I don't want her to feel weird around me. I need to be okay. I need to move on with my life. I need to be able to hold and enjoy someone else's baby."

Lonnie put his hand on my shoulder. "Lacy suggested you come to dinner on Sunday. It'll give the two of you time to visit and spend some time with the kids. I can't imagine what you're going through. I guess no one can who hasn't experienced what you have. But Lacy and I are here for you. Anything you need."

I smiled. "I'd like that. Really. But if I come to dinner, you have to promise you won't treat me like a piece of glass. I've had enough of the kid gloves treatment to last a lifetime."

"Got it. With my boys, I can promise glass isn't something that lasts long in our house anyway. I'll have Lacy call to set things up."

"I'm looking forward to it."

I was relieved to have this huge project to focus on, and now that we were getting details down on paper, I was even more excited and terrified. The success of this enterprise would depend on having the right person to run the inn, which I was afraid might be hard to do. The right person would be cheerful, organized, creative, and a master in the kitchen. He or she would need to have excellent customer service skills and be adept with finances. I hoped I'd find someone who would be as passionate about the inn as Lonnie was. I began to list the skills and personality traits I was looking for. I'd need someone experienced and mature, maybe fifty-five to sixty-five, a grandmotherly type looking for a second career as she eased into retirement. I'd begun to list additional attributes my perfect candidate would possess when Georgia Carter showed up at my door and my list went out the window.

"Are you Abby Sullivan?" A tiny pixie with huge blue eyes and long blond hair that looked like a halo under the setting sun asked when I answered the knock on my door.

"I am."

"I'm Georgia Carter, and this," the girl, who looked as if she couldn't be more than twenty-five but I suspected might be older, turned to the huge black dog beside her, "is Ramos."

I wondered why this girl and the dog, who had to outweigh her by a good fifty pounds, were standing on my front porch. I was about to ask when she continued.

"I spoke to Velma at the diner. She thought you might have a job, and maybe even a place for Ramos and me to stay."

"A job? I'm afraid there's been a misunderstanding. I don't have either, and while I do plan to turn the big house into an inn, we're months away from that."

Georgia looked at the big house. "You're going to open an inn?"

"Eventually."

"I'm an excellent cook and I'm good with people."

I paused as I considered my reply. "I will be hiring someone to cook and manage the inn, but as I said, I'm quite a while away from opening. I haven't even started the renovations yet."

"Which is another thing I'm here to inquire about. I don't have a contractor's license, but I've worked on a lot of crews and I'm good with a hammer."

I hesitated, unsure how to proceed.

"And I'll work cheap." Georgia looked at the ancient Ford truck I assumed she was driving. "Ramos and I have been on the road for a while. We've taken on odd jobs along the way, including the construction jobs I referred to. I'm a hard worker and I know I can do a good job for you, whatever you need me to do." She looked me in the eye. "Ramos and I just rolled into town and we really need a place to stay that will allow dogs."

I hesitated.

"Please. We've been on the road for over a year, but there's something about this place that feels right. Do you know what I mean?"

Actually, I did know what she meant. And I recognized the look in her eyes that, despite her outward cheerfulness, clearly communicated fatigue and despair.

"We can bunk anywhere," she added. "If there's a room in the house you plan to renovate that we can use for the time being, that would be great. I could sleep in my truck, but it's started to get cold at night."

"You said you've been on the road. Where are you from originally?"

"Boston. I lived within twenty miles of the house I grew up in until a year ago, when…" she hesitated, "when my world was turned upside down and I found myself broke, homeless, and suddenly single after seven years of marriage. I know you don't know me and you have no reason to help me, but I promise you that if you take a chance on me, I won't let you down."

I thought about the second bedroom in the cottage and my air mattress, which I'd no longer need now that I had a bed. "I've hired a general contractor to take care of the renovations in the main house, so you'll need to talk to him about a job, but I do have a spare room. You and Ramos are welcome to stay with me for a few days, at least while you sort everything out."

The girl's face lit up. "Thank you. You have no idea how much this means to us."

I did know how much it meant to her. While I hadn't ended up broke or homeless, I too had found my world shattered a year ago, and I'd been looking for a place to rebuild my life ever since. Perhaps Georgia and I were kindred spirits, meant to share a moment while we found a new footing. I stepped aside to allow her and her dog to enter the cottage. "Does Ramos like cats?"

Georgia looked around the room. "Ramos is fine with cats. Do you have one?"

Did I? I hadn't definitely decided to keep the cat, but I couldn't kick him out in the snow any more than I could leave this poor girl and her dog out in the cold. "For the time being," I finally answered as I realized my solitary life had suddenly become very crowded indeed.

******

Later that evening, I settled in with my laptop. I wasn't sure Annie would respond to my emails, but I'd given it some thought and decided that even if she didn't, I was still going to send them. She was my sister, after all, and despite everything between us, that would always be the case.

I knew Mama would want us to stay in touch. Sisters were God's way of ensuring we'd always have a friend. I suppose we were both to blame for the rift that had torn us apart, but I was finally at the point where I was willing to work past the part that was mine, if only she'd be willing to do the same with the part that was hers.

My fingers hovered above the keyboard as I contemplated where to start. I wasn't certain Annie would ever read this, so I'd keep it short. I could hear Rufus purring next to me. I found his presence gave me comfort and, in an odd way, the courage, to do what I needed to do. And it gave me a topic with which to begin.

Dear Annie,

You'll never believe this, but I've adopted a cat. Actually, the cat adopted me. His name is Rufus and he's huge. He's somewhat opinionated and pushy, but he's a real sweetie as well. I can't wait for you to meet him. He sort of reminds me of that old cat Mrs. Green had when we lived next door to her before Dad left. Of course, Rufus isn't full of the devil the way Mrs. Green's old cat was.

I hope you'll be able to come out and visit soon. I want to share my view with you, and I want you to see that I'm okay. I have an extra room, so you can stay as long as you want. Well, there's currently a homeless waif and a giant dog living in the extra room, but if you come, I'll make room for you.

Things with the house are going well. I've hired a general contractor to handle the remodel. I really think the place is going to be amazing. I've attached a few photos of the house and the town so you can start to get a feel for my new life. I have difficult moments every now and then, which is to be expected, but overall, I'm happy. Please be happy for me.

I love you,
Abby

Chapter 8

I woke to snow falling outside my window the following morning. I could hear Georgia moving around in the other room and considered getting up, but it was so snuggly here in my big new bed, cuddled up with Rufus, enjoying a few minutes of quiet. After I'd invited Georgia in the previous afternoon, I'd learned she'd married her college sweetheart after graduation and been blissfully happy for seven wonderful years, until her husband, a financial planner, was accused of swindling money from his customers. In the blink of an eye, she went from being happily married with her own home and business, to flat broke, homeless, and single after her husband committed suicide rather than go to prison.

I shared with her my own loss, and somewhere along the way, as the day turned to night and the clock passed the midnight hour, the two of us bonded. The longer Georgia and I talked, the more certain I was that she was exactly the sort of person I'd need to run the inn. The business she'd had before the bankruptcy that had followed her husband's conviction was a catering company, and while I'd yet to taste her food, I was confident she could cook. The fact that she'd run a successful business for five years told me she must be good with people and money, although I should check her references. She assured me she was willing to clean rooms and do the laundry in addition to the cooking, especially if there were just four rooms. We discussed having someone come in a couple of times a week to handle the larger chores.

I was fine with her staying with me in the cottage until the manager's suite was done, and with her having Ramos at the inn as long as he was well behaved and good with the guests. I supposed it was early to get too excited, but suddenly the world looked bright and hopeful.

"Wow, you've been busy," I said when I finally did get up and wander into the guesthouse's common area. The fire was dancing merrily and there was something wonderful smelling in the oven.

"I got up early to do something special to thank you for everything." Georgia handed me a mug filled with hot coffee. "Have a seat at the counter and I'll grab your breakfast."

"You made breakfast?" I slid onto a barstool and took a long, slow sip. I felt my body warm up just a bit as the hot liquid made its way down my throat and into my stomach.

Georgia pulled an egg dish from the oven. "I ran into town to get a few supplies. There's a breakfast casserole and a fresh fruit salad."

Be still my heart. That sounded amazing. And I was starving after mostly subsisting on sandwiches.

"That sounds wonderful, but you didn't have to do all that."

"I wanted to," Georgia said as she began filling plates. "Cooking relaxes me, and it's been a while since I've stayed anywhere with a kitchen."

She set a plate in front of me, and I took a bite and chewed slowly. "Delicious."

Georgia smiled. "I'm glad you like it. The kitchen is adequate and the view is amazing, but we need to get some pans and dishes. Unless you have some."

"I haven't had my things from San Francisco sent yet, so stocking the kitchen is on my list of things to do. I need to go into town to get the paint for the bathroom cabinets, and if you want to come along, we can drive to the home store in the next town to pick out some pans and other things."

Georgia hesitated. "I don't have much cash to pitch in."

I took another bite of the quiche. "Not a problem. For food like this, I'd be willing to pay for solid-gold baking pans."

Georgia grinned and took a bite of her own food. "Gold isn't practical or necessary. I'm sure we can get what we need for a reasonable price. I'll take Ramos out for a walk along the bluff after I eat, but after that I'm all yours."

"I'm going to jot down some notes for my new book and then head into the shower. Why don't we plan to go into town at around eleven?"

"Perfect."

******

We literally filled the back of my SUV with kitchen supplies, bedding, and towels and rugs for the bathroom, and then we went to the diner for a much-deserved meal. If Georgia was going to stay with me a while, she'd need a bed, but she'd slept on my air mattress the night before and had made it clear she was satisfied with that for the time being. Eventually, when the manager's suite was ready, I'd buy furniture for that space, the same as I would for the rest of the inn. The cottage had come mostly unfurnished when I bought it, other than the set of four barstools, an old sofa, and a few odds and ends in the kitchen. Georgia and I talked about making a trip back to the furniture store to look for a dining table and some additional furniture for the main living area. Maybe while we were there I'd buy a bed as well.

"Afternoon, Velma," I said as Georgia and I walked in from the road.

She looked up and smiled. "Sure is good to see the two of you together. I thought you might get along."

"I'm very grateful for the heads-up about the potential job." Georgia hugged the waitress, who was almost twice her height.

Velma glanced over Georgia's head and looked at me. "Figured you'd need some help with that big old house. Rufus with you?"

"He's at home with Ramos," I answered, sliding into a booth.

"Those two getting along okay?" Velma asked as she poured coffee into two mugs and set them on the table.

"Seem to be."

"Rufus is definitely the alpha of the two." Georgia chuckled as she slid into the booth across from me. "But Ramos doesn't mind. In fact, I think he enjoys getting bossed around a bit."

"Glad to hear that. Now, what can I get for you girls?"

I ordered a club sandwich, Georgia a cup of clam chowder. While we waited for our meals, we chatted about what we still needed to accomplish that afternoon. There wasn't room left in the cargo area of my SUV for much more, but I wanted to get the paint for the bathroom cabinets and figured I could fit it on the floor behind the seats. Then the only other stop to make was to the market to pick up a few staples for the kitchen.

Georgia chatted happily about a recipe she wanted to try while I sipped my coffee and let the festive scene outside the window warm my heart and soften the edges of my mending but still fragile soul. In many ways, I couldn't believe that after a year of struggle I'd finally found the solace I'd needed to make my life whole in this little town featuring streets with holiday names. Before the accident, I'd never considered living in a small town. I'd thrived on the hustle and bustle of the big city and could only imagine how boring a slower pace would be. Sure, I missed the stimulation of big-city life from time to time now, but after everything that had happened, a conversation about using ginger spice in place of cinnamon left me feeling just right.

"So, have you heard anything more about Darcy's murder?" I asked Velma after Georgia finished what she had to say and picked up her own coffee. The murdered girl had been in the back of my mind constantly since I'd heard of her death, and thinking about San Francisco had made me think about Ben, which made me think about murder investigations. Velma seemed to know a lot of people, which meant she'd be up on all the local news and gossip.

"The police have been interviewing some of her friends. Some of the customers at the bar on Saturday too. Everyone agrees she left alone, but no one seems to know where she went."

"I heard the police were talking to Darcy's boyfriend and her best friend," I said.

"They spoke to Carly, the best friend, but as of the last time I spoke to Colt, he hadn't been able to locate Adam."

"Do they think something happened to him as well?" I asked.

Velma shrugged. "There's a lot of speculation, but no one knows for sure. He shared a small house in town with a roommate who told Colt he hadn't seen Adam since Saturday afternoon."

"So he could be a second victim," Georgia said, her tone breathy.

"Could be," Velma answered. "But so far, his body hasn't turned up. There are some folks who are starting to say he might be the one who killed Darcy."

I raised a brow. "You don't say. Why do folks suspect that?"

"It seems they were having problems and had actually broken up the weekend before the murder. Or at least that's the rumor."

"If it's true they broke up, maybe they weren't ever together on Saturday night," I pointed out.

"Maybe not. Although if Adam isn't wrapped up in Darcy's disappearance in some way, where did he go off to?"

Good question.

"I know Colt talked to Wayne Newman," Velma continued, "the bartender who worked with Darcy the night she died. I don't think the police suspect him of any wrongdoing, but if Darcy had plans that night that ended up getting her killed, she might have mentioned them to him. They were pretty tight. Wayne was quite a bit older than Darcy—about twenty-five years older—but it seemed she looked at him as a father figure."

"She didn't have an actual father in her life?"

Velma shook her head. "He's in prison. Has been since she was a little girl."

"Really? What did he do?"

"Killed a man while committing a robbery. It was such a shame and so very pointless. Some poor guy was working the graveyard shift at a liquor store up the coast, never imagining a drugged-out junkie looking for some cash to get a fix would end his life before the evening was over."

"So Darcy's father was a drug addict?"

Velma nodded. "A functioning one. He somehow managed to hold down a job, but everyone knew he used drugs on a regular basis, and not just pot. He was in to the hard stuff. I'm not sure how much it affected Darcy. She was only two or maybe three when he went to prison. Still, I guess growing up knowing your father was a killer would be a tough thing to deal with."

Yes, I supposed it would. "I stopped by the Reindeer Roundup for a pint yesterday and spoke to the man who was tending bar. He told me he was in the bar throwing darts on the night Darcy died."

"Must have been Denver Thomas," Velma said.

"Yes, that's right. Thomas mentioned a group of men in the bar on Saturday night who were headed north. One of them got handsy with Darcy, and when she rebuked him, he gave her a look Thomas interpreted to mean he wasn't *done with her* yet."

Velma frowned. "I wonder if Denver told that to Colt."

I shrugged. "He was pretty rude when I asked him about it, but I suppose he might talk to the chief of police if asked. A man passing through with a bellyful of alcohol and an interest in the victim sounds like a good suspect to me."

"Yeah, me too," Velma agreed.

"You said Darcy worked in a bar," Georgia joined in. "Did she have a substance abuse problem too?"

Velma shook her head. "Darcy didn't do drugs and she only drank socially, which was, I believe, at the root of the problem she was having with Adam. They'd been together for a while, but Adam was in to amphetamines. Still, if she was meeting him that night, he would have picked her up at the bar. Her leaving on foot doesn't make a bit of sense. Not only was it late, it was cold. Seems someone would have given her a ride if she didn't have her own car for some reason."

"Maybe she didn't mean to walk far," I suggested. "Maybe someone picked her up on the street, or she had plans to meet someone nearby."

"Maybe. Whatever her plans, they sure didn't work out for her."

No, they didn't. I was fairly cautious these days, but I could remember walking home from a bar or club when I was in my early twenties and I lived in a much more potentially dangerous neighborhood than quaint and friendly Holiday Bay.

Velma looked toward the counter. "Your lunch is up."

"Knowing a young woman was killed right here in Holiday Bay makes me doubly glad I'm not still living in my truck," Georgia said.

"You do have your big dog for protection," I said.

"Ramos looks like he'd make a formidable opponent, but he's just a big teddy bear. Heck, he's afraid of your cat."

"True. And I agree it's frightening to think there could be a killer walking around here. When I spoke to Denver Thomas yesterday, he seemed positive the killer was someone passing through. And maybe it was. But I don't think I'll feel completely safe until we know for sure."

"Yeah. Me neither."

Georgia and I dug into our food. We were halfway through when a tall man with dark hair wearing a police uniform came in. He glanced at us, then went to the counter.

"You're late," Velma said.

"I'm not here to eat." He handed Velma a photo. "Have you seen this girl?"

She studied the photo, then shook her head. "I can't say as I have. Is she involved in Darcy's murder?"

"We don't know. This photo of the two of them was posted to Darcy's social media account about an hour after she left the bar the night she died."

"What do you think that means?"

"I'm not sure," he answered. "From the crowd in the background, it looks as if they were at a party when the photo was taken."

Velma looked at it again. "I don't recognize anyone else either. Seems like an older crowd, though."

"No one else I've spoken to recognizes anyone standing behind them, so I'm thinking this party wasn't in town, or at least that the guests were visitors."

"Denver Thomas told me there was a group of men from out of town in the bar on Saturday night and one of them showed particular interest in Darcy," I said.

Velma gestured to Georgia and me. "This is Abby Sullivan, and that's Georgia Carter."

He glanced at me. "Were you in the bar on Saturday night?"

"No, but I stopped by yesterday. Apparently, the men were all drinking heavily. One in particular showed interest in Darcy. At least according to Denver Thomas."

He crossed the room and handed me the photo. "Do you recognize anyone?"

"The girl in the red jacket."

"That's Darcy Jared. When did you last see her?"

"I didn't see her exactly; I saw a photo of her. A bunch of photos of her, in a box with a lot of other things in the basement in my house, although she had blond hair, not brown, in them. Still, I'm sure it's her."

"Darcy bleached her hair for a while a few years ago," Velma said.

He frowned. "Yes, she did. What house are you talking about?"

"The bluff house," Velma answered in my stead. "Abby bought the place. Lonnie's going to renovate it, and Georgia here is going to help her turn it into an inn."

"Is this box still at your house?" he asked.

I nodded.

He looked at his watch. "I have an appointment with Darcy's cousin. Would it be all right if I came out there in about two hours to take a look at what you have?"

"Fine by me. The box is in the basement of the main house, along with other similar ones, but I'm living in the cottage. Come get me there when you arrive and I'll show you where it is."

"I'll do that. And thanks." He took the photo and left.

"Who was that?" Georgia asked.

"Colt Wilder. I guess I should have introduced him. He's the chief of police."

"He's quite the babe," Georgia said as she continued to look toward the door.

Velma chuckled. "That he is."

Chapter 9

Chief Colt Wilder arrived at the house just about two hours after we'd run into him at the diner. I called out to Georgia to let her know I was going to meet him, grabbed a jacket, and went out to meet his car.

"So, you're going to turn this old place into an inn," he said conversationally.

"I'm going to try. Lonnie Parker seems to think we can."

"Lonnie's the best. If he's working with you, the place will be fantastic."

The snow had started up again, so I took a red knit cap out of my pocket and pulled it onto my head. "Lacy told me the two of you are friends."

"We are. I was the best man at his wedding."

"He and Lacy seem really great. All the Parkers seem great. I haven't met the older three boys, but Lacy invited me to Sunday dinner, so I'll have the chance then."

I used my key to unlock the back door, which led into the kitchen. I hadn't locked the basement door after I'd found the boxes, so I opened it and reached for the light.

"It looks like someone might have been hiding out in here," Wilder said, looking at the mattress.

"You think so? I just figured the mattress had been discarded by the previous owner when he moved."

"Perhaps." Wilder crossed to the boxes.

"There are four boxes, each containing random items and an envelope with photos," I said. "The subjects in the photos in each box are different. All female, and all young. I figured the boxes must have been left behind by a previous resident too. The one with the photos of Darcy is to the right."

Wilder pulled on gloves and opened the lid of the box I'd indicated. He sorted through the items inside, then pulled out the envelope. "These look like things that would belong to a high school student. The photos are dated as well." He sifted through the photos. "The boxes are pretty dusty. I assume they've been here for a while." Wilder picked up a photo. "This was taken at the harvest festival when Darcy was in high school, and the one after at a high school football game, also when she was a student."

"How can you be sure they were taken then?"

"Darcy has naturally brown hair, but she bleached it when she was in high school. She has blond hair in all these photos, and she has her cheerleader uniform on in one." Wilder paused at a photo of the girl standing in the snow. "Did you touch these?"

"Yes. I didn't realize who the girl was at the time."

He put them back in the box, then turned to the one on the left.

"Do you know that girl?" I asked, as he studied the dark-haired subject, who was sitting on a bench overlooking the sea.

"Karen Stinson. She was found dead in the river at the bottom of the falls this past July. Everyone assumed she'd been hiking, slipped, and fell."

I felt a chill run down my spine. "Do you think the same person who killed Darcy killed Karen?"

"Maybe." He continued to look through the photos. "I didn't know Karen as well as I knew Darcy, but I imagine these photos were also taken several years ago at least." Wilder stuffed the photos of Karen back into the envelope and opened the third box. He took out the photos and winced. "Well, I'll be damned."

"What is it?" I asked.

He held up the photo of a third young girl standing in front of a Ferris wheel. It was dark, but you could see a carnival in the background. "Carrie Long. She disappeared in the middle of the night this past September."

"And the photos? Do they seem to have been taken several years ago as well?"

Wilder nodded. "It looks like she was still in high school."

I didn't like where this was going. "Is there a fourth girl?" I asked as he opened the last box.

"Tracy Edwards," Wilder answered as he glared at a photo of another young woman.

"And what happened to her?" I asked.

Wilder's lips tightened. "Nothing. At least nothing has yet. I just saw her in town this morning." He took out his phone, pushed a button, and waited for someone on the other end to pick up. "I need you to pick up Tracy Edwards. Take her to my office and have her wait for me." Wilder hung up, then looked at me. "I'm going to take the boxes with me. We might get lucky and lift a print. Because you touched things, I'll need you to come by the station to have your prints taken. That way we can eliminate them right off the bat."

"I'd be happy to. Do you want me to come at any particular time?"

"Any time before six would be great."

He turned and looked around the basement. "If someone was here recently, there might be physical evidence to find, although from the age of the photos and the amount of dust on the boxes, I'm sticking with my initial impression that the boxes have been here for several years at least. Still, I'm going to tape off the entry and send a team over. You can leave the back door open or be available to let them in."

"I should be around. I'll give you my cell number."

Wilder led me back toward the stairs. As we passed the mattress, I felt another chill run down my spine. Had the person who killed Darcy been staying here at some point? And if so, might they come back?

After Wilder left, I went back to the cottage to fill Georgia in. As I had been, she was shocked and concerned. Who wouldn't feel somewhat vulnerable? I glanced at Georgia's Ramos and found I was grateful for his massive presence, even though he probably wouldn't be much of a guard dog. I decided to take care of the fingerprints right away. It was already past four and I didn't want to become distracted with something else and forget. Georgia chose to remain at the cottage and continue organizing the kitchen. She'd also need to take Ramos for a walk before dark.

The Holiday Bay Police Station was located in an old brick building between the tiny library and the post office. This was the part of town I'd heard referred to as the public annex. The ground was covered with snow, but from a photo I'd seen, I knew beneath it was a lawn where free concerts were held in the summer.

A middle-aged woman with a rounded figure and a purple tint to her hair greeted me as I entered the station. "You must be Abby Sullivan."

"I am," I confirmed.

"Peach Sherwood. I've heard so much about you."

"You have?"

She stood up and came around the desk and took my hand. "Velma said you bought the house on the bluff, but she didn't tell me you were such a pretty little thing." Peach frowned. "You aren't Abagail Sullivan the writer, are you?"

I nodded.

"Well, if that doesn't take all. I'm such a huge fan. I'm pretty sure I've read all your romances, even the steamy ones."

I smiled. "I'm happy you enjoyed them."

"I heard you'd stopped writing after the death of your family. I'm very sorry for your loss."

"Thank you." I could feel tension build in my chest. "I'm here to have my fingerprints taken. Did Chief Wilder tell you I'd be in?"

"He did. Just give me a minute and we'll take care of that for you." She turned on a machine. "I can't believe Abagail Sullivan is right here in our station.

101

Does the fact that you're opening an inn mean you've given up writing for good?"

"No. I'm working on a thriller. Will this take long?"

"Just a few minutes. Everything is digitized these days. You don't even have to get your fingers dirty. You will need to wash your hands before we do the prints, though, so they're free of any lotions. The washroom is just through that door."

Happy to have a reason to escape, I headed toward the washroom, even though I didn't have any lotion on my hands. I'd hoped it would take longer for the locals to figure out who I was. I should have realized it was only a matter of time before my sad little story was out to everyone, and they started looking at me with pity in their eyes. Maybe I should have changed my name before moving to Holiday Bay. It was too late for that now.

Taking a deep breath to calm the panic that was building, I washed my hands and returned to where Peach was waiting for me.

She took my hand. "This won't take long at all. Just relax your hand and let me place your fingers."

The sky had darkened and the lights along the main avenue were lit up by the time I returned to my SUV. It was beginning to look like a fairyland. I couldn't wait for the Christmas Festival to get underway. I was sure it would be magical. I considered stopping by the small holiday store I'd seen on an earlier trip into town to pick up a few decorations for the cottage. Nothing too over the top. Maybe some lights and a few pieces of garland, and a couple of candles for atmosphere. I was standing near my vehicle, debating whether to make the stop now or at a later time when I saw Colt Wilder walking toward me.

"Are you here to get your prints done?"

"Just finished up."

"Thank you for being so prompt."

"I'm happy to help out in any way I can. Did you speak to Tracy?"

"We did. She's going to stay with some relatives on the West Coast until we figure out what's going on."

"Did she know anything about the box with her belongings in it?"

"It was part of a time capsule project her graduating class did. Four years ago, every senior was given a box in which to place items that were significant to their time in high school. The boxes were locked in the school basement. The idea was that they'd be opened at the class's ten-year reunion."

"Obviously someone pilfered the boxes."

"Obviously," Wilder said in a deep voice. "I called the school. They're going to do an inventory. I'll be very interested in hearing whether there are other boxes missing."

"Other missing boxes could indicate other girls in danger," I realized.

"Yes."

I wiped a snowflake from my face. "I wonder why the boxes we found were in the basement of my house."

"I suppose it was as good a hiding place as any. No one has lived in that house for a very long time."

"Lonnie told me Bodine Devine moved out of the house about three years ago. The girls graduated four years ago. You don't think…"

Wilder frowned. "Perhaps I should give Devine a call."

Chapter 10

As he said he would, Chief Wilder had sent someone to tape off the basement and verified that it would be fine to start work in the rest of the house on Monday. I'd asked him if he had any news about Darcy's murder he could share with me, and his response was that he was "working on it." Vague, but I understood. Ben hadn't liked to talk about his active cases either. Still, my curiosity had been piqued, so I decided to do some digging of my own.

"Are you still looking into the murder of that poor girl they found in the woods?" Georgia asked me when I'd settled down at the dining table we'd purchased, along with a bed for Georgia, a sofa, two armchairs to frame the fireplace, and a beautiful walnut coffee table.

"The more I look, the more fascinated I become. I suspect whoever killed Darcy might be responsible for two other deaths, though it's important to look at Darcy as a victim in isolation as well."

Georgia sat down across from me. "What have you found?"

"Darcy was the youngest of five girls, all raised by their mother alone after their father was arrested. It seems all her sisters have gone on to live conservative, productive lives. Two, both college graduates, have successful careers and have left Maine. Michelle, the oldest sister, is thirty-five, married to a local pastor, and still lives in Holiday Bay. Kendall, the sister closest in age to Darcy at twenty-four, is engaged to Wesley, the oldest son of Patrice and Jasper Hamilton, the heir to the Hamilton estate."

Georgia popped a piece of the cookie she'd been nibbling in her mouth. "I've never heard of the Hamiltons."

"Jasper Hamilton is the founder of Holiday Bay Community Bank. I don't get the sense the family is super rich, like the Hiltons or one of those families, but from what I've found, they have more money than either of us ever will."

Georgia laughed. "If you're comparing his fortune to the amount of money I'll ever have, that's setting the bar pretty low. Are you talking about the huge house up on the hill that looks a lot like a castle?"

"Yes. That's the one."

Georgia put another piece of her cookie into her mouth. "Okay. Despite their father being a drugged-out killer, Darcy had four sisters who seem to have done well for themselves. Is that relevant?"

"I'm not sure," I admitted. "I mostly set out to look for possible motives if Darcy's death turned out not to have been committed by someone just passing through town. The church where Steven Fisher is pastor is pretty conservative, and from what I've been able to deduce, Darcy was very much the opposite."

"So you think Darcy was killed because she worked in a bar and had a wild side?" Georgia asked.

"Not necessarily. Right now I'm just gathering data. It does seem as if Darcy might have been the least ambitious and successful of her siblings, though. I'm not saying anyone would kill her because of that, I'm just saying it's interesting."

Georgia got up to pour herself a cup of coffee before sitting back down across from me. "How do you know how to find all this stuff?"

"First, I'm a writer, and we have to do a lot of research. Along the way, I've learned tricks to find the information I need. And I was married to a detective. He had mad investigative skills he shared with me. And I have a friend with connections. His help is invaluable when I need information that isn't accessible to the average human being."

"Friend?"

"My husband's old roommate. He ended up working for the FBI, and Ben and I stayed in touch with him after he moved to DC. Ben called him a few times over the years for help on one case or another."

"And he'd help you too?" Georgia asked.

I got up to refill my own cup. "He would. Unless it's hugely top secret or something. In the case of Darcy Jared, if I can manage to come up with a viable theory and need some information, I think he might come through for me. After Ben died, he called me and said he'd always be there for me, and if I needed anything, just ask."

Georgia laughed. "I like your style, Abby Sullivan. I'm going to take Ramos out for a walk.

When I get back, we can go over the grocery list. I thought I'd run into town and get the supplies we need for the week while you singlehandedly solve Darcy's murder while writing the next *New York Times* best-selling mystery."

I grinned. "Don't for a minute think I'm not going to do exactly that."

After Georgia went out with Ramos, I began to see what I could find out about the other two girls. I knew their names and that they were in the same graduating class, but nothing else.

Karen Stinson was found dead in a nearby river this past July. Until the items in the basement had been discovered, her death had been considered an accident. She was twenty-two and worked at the local preschool. She was single, and based on what I could find out by searching her social media accounts, she had a fair number of friends, though she rarely dated. From the photos I found, she liked to hike and kayak. Comments posted to her Facebook timeline after her death made it appear she was well liked and respected. It appeared she'd been quiet, preferring nature to partying, but to know more, I'd have to confirm that with friends or others who knew her. I scoured her social media accounts in search of information about her family. It took a while, but eventually I found a photo in which she'd been tagged. Also tagged were two young women who looked a lot like her who were identified as sisters.

After an hour of research, I had a profile of sorts. Karen was born in a small town in Indiana. Her father died when she was young and she was raised by her mother. Being raised by a single mom provided a common link with Darcy. When Karen was ten, she and her mother moved to Holiday Bay, and it seemed she'd lived here until her death.

Carrie Long, also twenty-two when she went missing, had never been found. From what I could find online, it appeared she was a single mom with a one-year-old. She'd worked as a cashier at the market and volunteered at the day care center in exchange for babysitting for her daughter when she was at work. She was a parishioner at the community church and had been dating a young man named Grayson Porter, who was twenty-five and a youth minister working on his master's degree in theology.

What did Darcy, a waitress with a wild side, a preschool teacher with a love of nature, and a single mom have in common? On the surface, not a lot, except for the fact that they went to the same high school, so most likely knew each other. I was just about to Google Tracy when my phone rang.

It was Lacy, reminding me about dinner tomorrow night. "Lonnie told me about the boxes and mattress you found in the basement," she segued into what I suspected was the real reason for her call pretty quickly. "How freaky is that?"

"Pretty freaky. You've lived in Holiday Bay for a long time. Did you know Karen Stinson and Carrie Long?"

"Sure. Carrie attended the same church Lonnie and I do. She was such a sweet person. So open and giving. She was raising her daughter all on her own after the man she'd been dating dumped her when he found out she was pregnant, but she never complained for a minute. She worked hard and she loved that baby. I don't know what happened to her, but I do know she wouldn't just take off the way some people said."

"There are those who think she ran away?" I asked, then waited for Lacy to reply.

"A few people, including the detective from the county who came to investigate. They say she was under a lot of stress in the days before she disappeared. She had a full-time job at the market, plus she helped out at the day care almost full-time hours to cover childcare for her daughter. She really had a lot on her plate, and there were some people close to her who told the detective she was pretty much at the end of her rope. On the night she disappeared, she called a neighbor to come over to stay with the baby, told her a friend had called in a panic after their car broke down and she needed to go pick them up. The baby was sleeping, and Carrie promised to be no more than thirty minutes. She never came back."

"And her car?"

"They never found it. Her cell phone either. Or her purse, for that matter. She just disappeared. I know they used phone records to try to identify the friend who called her for the ride, but it turned out she didn't get a call from anyone before she called the neighbor to come over. At least she didn't get a call on her cell or the landline in her home."

Okay, that was strange. She left her daughter with a neighbor in the middle of the night in response to a call for help from a friend, but there was no record of that call. If not for the photos in the basement, which seemed to indicate she could have been selected the same as Karen and Darcy, who were dead, I might think she'd taken off as well.

"Carrie loved her daughter," Lacy continued. "She wouldn't have just left her if she had a choice. I always felt she couldn't have simply run away."

"Were there any other indicators that she might have?" I asked. "Had she cleaned out her bank account or taken a leave from her job?"

Lacy didn't answer.

"Lacy? Are you still there?"

"I'm here. And yes, there were other indicators. She'd taken a large amount of money out of her savings account the week before. The bank manager questioned her at the time, and Carrie said she was helping out a friend. She didn't have a lot of money, and the bank manager said he tried to counsel her not to draw her account down so low, but she did it anyway, and it wasn't his business what she did with her money."

Withdrawing most of her cash and leaving to help out a friend who they couldn't prove called would lead to the conclusion that someone had simply taken off to start a new life. "What can you tell me about Karen Stinson?"

"Karen worked at the preschool the twins attend. The boys went there too, and all the kids absolutely adored her. Karen was sweet and thoughtful and patient. Everyone said she really enjoyed her students."

"I heard she fell to her death while hiking."

"Maybe. She was the outdoorsy sort. She liked to hike and ski and she often went off alone, which I didn't understand. If it were me, I'd find a hiking buddy, but people said she was a bit of a loner when she wasn't working. When she ended up dead in the river, no one thought much about it. Everyone figured she fell and, being alone, there was no one to help her."

"Did she drown?" I asked.

"Colt told Lonnie there was water in her lungs, but she suffered a head injury when she fell that probably caused her to pass out."

Suddenly the image of a head injury caused by blunt force trauma, not a fall, popped into my mind.

"Tracy is alive, but there were photos of her in the basement too. Can you tell me about her?"

"She lived here with her family when she was young. She must have been in seventh or eighth grade when her parents divorced, and after high school she and her mother moved out west. I'm not sure where exactly. She came back to Holiday Bay last summer, got a job working for one of the novelty shops in town, but I think that was seasonal. I think she works part time at Gilda's place."

I remembered Gilda owned one of the other diners.

"I don't know Tracy as well as the others," Lacy said, "but she seems nice enough. She always has a smile on her face. If you're really curious, you can ask Gilda about her, at Gilda's Café on Easter Avenue."

"I haven't met her yet, but Velma's mentioned her to me. I'll have to stop by."

"Velma is open for breakfast and lunch and Gilda is open for lunch and dinner. If you do go for dinner, have the pot roast. It's excellent."

"I'll do that."

"But not tomorrow," Lacy reminded me. "Tomorrow you're coming here for lasagna."

"I wouldn't miss it for the world."

I'd been about to look into Tracy's background when Lacy called, but now I found I was more interested in what had happened to Carrie. I was able to find quite a bit about her, including that she was, as Lacy had said, an active member of their church. I surfed around a bit more until I found a mention in the local paper about Carrie's dad who, interestingly enough, was also in prison. The same prison as Darcy's dad? I wondered. I made a note to talk to Chief Wilder about two of the four fathers. I was about to widen my search when I heard a car pull up. I assumed it was Georgia and logged off to help her with the groceries. I'd given her money to pick up everything we'd need for a week at least, so she'd have a lot to bring in, sort through, and put away. As I greeted her and grabbed the first two of the truckful of bags, I let my mind wander to the mystery that had grabbed my attention. Wilder seemed competent. I was sure he didn't need me digging around in his business. Still, perhaps I'd treat us both to dinner at Gilda's. Maybe the longtime local could provide insight into the comings and goings of all four girls, but particularly Tracy, who'd worked for her part time.

******

Like Velma's, Gilda's Café was saturated with warmth and small-town charm. As Lacy had suggested, I ordered the pot roast, and Georgia chose the chicken. The waitress who took our order was a teenager, so I asked to speak to Gilda when she had a moment.

"This place is so cute and cozy," Georgia said when the waitress left to get our beverages. "I love all the fall decorations. The little Thanksgiving Village is very quaint, although I suppose with Thanksgiving coming up in just a few days, it will be replaced by a Christmas Village by the next time we come in."

"It's almost Thanksgiving?" I gasped.

Georgia chuckled. "It's the fourth Thursday in November, where it's been waiting all this time."

"Seems early."

"Actually, it is this year. I thought I'd make a turkey and all the trimmings. Is there someone you'd like to invite?"

Was there? Not really. "I think it'll be nice to have a quiet day. I don't know anyone well enough yet to invite them to a holiday meal and the cottage is pretty small. Maybe we can build a fire and watch holiday movies on the Hallmark Channel."

"We'll need cable for that," Georgia said.

"I'll have cable installed. If I call on Monday, they may be able to get it hooked up by Wednesday."

"Sounds like fun. Were you thinking of decorating the cottage?"

"Yes," I decided quickly. "I've been meaning to do it. We can get some candles and garlands for the mantel, and maybe a little tree for the window near the dining table. I didn't bring any decorations with me, but we can go into town and buy some. There's a holiday store in town and several shops on Christmas Boulevard with signs announcing decorations for sale."

Georgia smiled. "Suddenly, I'm looking forward to a holiday I felt I'd never be able to enjoy again."

When the waitress delivered our meals she said Gilda was excited to meet us and would be happy to come by, but Saturday was a busy night for her and she didn't think she'd have time to take a break until almost closing. She suggested we come to the back to talk while she cooked, and we decided to at least go back to say hello when we finished eating. If Gilda was swamped, we didn't want to bother her; we could return another time.

"Gilda," I said when we ducked into the kitchen, making sure to stay well back and out of the way, "I'm Abby Sullivan and this is Georgia Carter."

Gilda, who was as short as Velma was tall, and as plump as Velma was thin, smiled at us. "I've heard so much about both of you. I'm glad you finally made it in. I'm sorry I can't take a break, but I'm shorthanded tonight."

"Not a problem," Georgia said, "and we don't want to get in your way. We really just wanted to meet you and let you know how amazing our dinner was."

She grinned. "I'm glad you liked it. Velma told me you're a cook yourself."

Georgia nodded. "I am. Or at least I will be again when the inn opens. The pies you have on display look truly amazing. I'll need to come back sometime to try a piece."

"We're open eleven thirty to nine. Hopefully, I'll have found a replacement for Tracy by then and can really visit."

"I heard one of the girls with a box in my basement worked for you," I jumped in, spotting an opening.

"She did, and I hope she will again when the police figure things out and she can come back. When I heard what had been found, I was shocked. Shocked, I tell you. This is a nice little town. Things like whatever appears to be going on don't happen here."

I guess I understood the attitude a lot of the locals seemed to have.

"I feel odd about the fact that the boxes were found in a house that belongs to me. Not that I've owned it very long, but still…"

"I'm glad you bought the place and found the boxes. If you hadn't, Colt might not have been able to warn Tracy in time. That girl has already been through so much in her short life. She deserves to have things go her way for once."

"I understand she only moved back to Holiday Bay this past summer," I said.

"That's right. Just this past June. Then to have something like this happen only a few months later. What is this world coming to?"

We chatted for a few more minutes, then took a walk around the little town. The festive atmosphere went a long way toward helping me find my holiday spirit. It was amazing what a difference a year could make.

Chapter 11

Georgia was baking something that smelled wonderful. Cookies, I thought. I could pick up a hint of both cinnamon and ginger. It was snowing again, so it seemed the perfect sort of day to settle in and get some work done. Georgia was staying in the bedroom at the front of the cottage that would eventually be my office, so I'd set up a desk for my computer in my bedroom. I'd spent the entire morning attempting to outline my novel. I had a general idea of where I wanted to go with it, as well as a vague feel for the main characters, but so far that old familiar itch to start writing hadn't quite grabbed me.

I'd thought I was ready to get back to work when I'd called Kate, but perhaps my phone call had been premature. I'd begun my writing career with sweet romances, which provided a natural segue into women's fiction. I enjoyed writing about the ups and downs of everyday life, but at some point I'd grown bored with what I felt were similar stories told from different angles and tried my hand at mystery. My work in the genre had served me well, but my world had changed, and as it had morphed into a new reality, so had I.

I needed a challenge. Something different. I thought a psychological thriller would fit the bill, but now I wasn't so certain. Maybe I should return to my roots and try a romance. Or a family drama? I'd been playing around with an idea for a multigenerational family all living in one house. The theme of family was a big one for me at the moment, although the family I had left had been reduced to a sister who refused to speak to me. Perhaps the hole in my life where a family once was had created a need to explore the complex relationships that came from being part of a large, close-knit group.

I tried a few ideas, but after making several attempts at an opening paragraph, I opened my mail app. I still hadn't heard from Annie, but that didn't mean I was going to stop trying to get through to her.

Dear Annie,

Can you believe it's almost Thanksgiving? I hope you and James have a wonderful holiday. Last year I was such a mess, I barely noticed the day, but I find I'm looking forward to a nice quiet dinner this year with my new roommate, my giant cat, and her even larger dog.

Did I tell you there's been a murder here in Holiday Bay? No need to worry about me; it has nothing to do with me, but I do find myself being drawn into the mystery. You know how I loved to help Ben with his cases. We made such a good team. I miss the long nights spent building theory until fatigue prevented either of us from forming another coherent thought.

The plans for the remodel are coming along nicely. I've been spending a lot of time thinking about building materials and color schemes. Did I mention I spoke to Kate? I've decided it's time to go back to work and have even started on a new novel.

I need to run as I have a full day ahead. I just wanted you to know I love and miss you.

Abby

I hit the Send button even as the little voice in the back of my mind nagged that I'd intentionally insinuated that my new novel was farther along than it was. Annie would be happy I was writing again. At least I think she would be. These days I had no idea what she was thinking. I logged back onto my computer and opened the file I'd begun to build on the four girls whose possessions and photos I'd found in the boxes in the basement. I wasn't sure why I was so fascinated with them. I'd never met any of them, and my connection to this town was very new. Still, I found myself being drawn in deeper, thinking about them whenever I had an odd minute.

After quite a bit of research, I felt I was beginning to get a feel for each of the young women. Darcy had been fun and social. Karen was outdoorsy and athletic. The main focus of Carrie's life was her daughter. I'd stumbled onto some photos of the baby and felt a pull on my heart. I was a mother without a baby and, apparently, Carrie's daughter was a baby without a mother. Life could be so cruel. More than anything, I wanted to figure out what had become of the young mother. She'd worked hard to provide for her baby, and I agreed with the people in the community who didn't believe she would just up and leave her daughter in the middle of the night. I even toyed with the idea that she could still be alive. She'd only been missing for two months and her body hadn't been found. The longer I looked at photos of that baby, the more urgent was my need to find out what had happened to Carrie. If Ben were here, he'd know what to do. He always did.

I closed my eyes and asked myself what Ben would do. If he were investigating this case, what would be his next move? The only links I had were that all four girls had gone to the same high school, had graduated the same year. Maybe whatever was driving the killer had originated there. High school was a tumultuous time. Maybe the person who took the boxes was a nerdy guy who'd been turned down by all four of them. Maybe it was a peer who wanted to be part of the popular crowd but couldn't quite make it. Maybe it was a teacher or staff person with a sick appetite for young girls. All of the girls had been exceptionally beautiful.

Making a quick decision, I logged onto the school website and downloaded a yearbook from four years ago. I found the senior class. Then I printed off the photos for the senior class, as well as for the people who'd worked at the school that year. I was having dinner with Lonnie and Lacy that evening. They were older than these girls, but they would probably recognize which of the students and staff still lived in the area. I wasn't sure the high school was the link to Darcy's murder, Karen's accident, and Carrie's disappearance I was looking for, but it was a good place to start, especially given the fact that the boxes I'd found had been stolen from the high school at some point after the senior class had stored them there.

When the pages had printed I took a shower to get ready for my dinner with the Parkers. I hoped I could get through the whole visit with their six children without breaking down.

******

Lonnie and Lacy had added Christmas lights to the eaves of their home since I was there. The effect was charming. The recent snow was marred with a lopsided snowman in need of some TLC and a whole lot of footprints in a variety of sizes. I smiled at the snowman as it seemed to wink at me with a dark pebble for an eye. The other one must have fallen out at some point. Georgia had made a yummy-looking cheesecake for me to bring to share with the family, as well as a box filled with chocolate chip cookies for any little Parkers who might not appreciate the rich taste of the creamy dessert.

"You brought dessert." Lacy beamed. "And it looks delicious."

"The cheesecake and cookies are a gift from my new roommate, Georgia."

"I heard someone moved in with you. You should have brought her with you tonight. I should have called and invited her myself."

"I'll introduce you sometime soon. I think you'll really like her. As for tonight, she seemed content settling down with my cat, her dog, and an old movie."

Lacy sighed. "I remember what it was like to have a solitary night at home with a glass of wine and a good book. It's been a while, but I remember." Lacy took my jacket and hung it up on a peg near the door. "Let's go into the kitchen. I'm just finishing up the lasagna. When I get it in the oven, we'll have a glass of wine and visit for a bit."

I sat down at the counter while Lacy finished assembling our dinner. "Your house looks lovely. The decorations are perfect for this space."

"Thanks. My decorating style has been somewhat fluid in recent years. When Lonnie and I first married, I was all about class. Our first Christmas tree as a married couple was decorated in red and gold. That was it, just red and gold. We also had a white tree with black ornaments and a teacup tree, which was basically just a fir with teacups hung on it. Then we had the triplets. I wanted our tree to have more of a family feel, so we did a traditional green and red one with ornaments for each boy. Then the twins came and the boys started preschool. When they came home with homemade ornaments, our tree needed to change again. Now we have a hodgepodge, but I love it. Most everything we put up has meaning for us."

"That's really nice. I noticed Sadie has her own wreath with her name on it."

"Sadie is part of the family." Lacy held up a bottle. "Is cabernet okay?"

"Cabernet is fine."

Lacy poured two glasses, then we went into the somewhat cluttered but spotlessly clean living room.

"Where are the kids?" I asked.

"The older five are in the den watching a Disney movie. The baby is napping. I should get her up in a few minutes, but I have time to drink my wine and talk for a while. Any news on the mystery I've begun to think of as 'The Case of the Boxes in the Basement'?"

I smiled. "I love that title. I may have to use it for a book."

Lacy smiled. "Be my guest."

"I wish I could say I've cracked the case, but I haven't. I'm focusing on the high school link for a bit." I grabbed an envelope with the photos I'd printed from my bag. "I printed out the class photos of the students and the staff the year all four girls graduated. I hoped you and Lonnie could look through them. Maybe we can narrow down who's still around."

"So you think the key is the high school?"

I shrugged. "Honestly, I have no idea, but it's a good place to start. On the surface, it doesn't appear the girls had a lot in common after they left high school. Karen was outdoorsy, Carrie had a baby, Darcy enjoyed the nightlife, and Tracy only recently returned to Holiday Bay. If there's someone who can be identified as a common denominator among them, it seems to me that person might have come into contact with them in high school."

"I agree. Lonnie is working on something out in the refinishing shed. I'll get him and we can look at the photos together."

Once Lacy returned with Lonnie, we sat down around the kitchen table. We went through the pages of photos slowly and put an X through the photos of anyone they knew for certain was no longer in town, circled the ones who were here, and put a small question mark next to anyone they weren't sure about. We came up with twenty-two students and twelve staff who were still around and eight students and two staff we needed to check on one way or another.

"It seems like a lot of the students left," I observed.

"There isn't a lot here for most," Lonnie said. "Those who have the grades and means go to college. Once they're gone, they seldom come back."

"Of the twenty-two students we know are still around, eight are male. My gut tells me the person who stole the boxes is a man. Do any of these eight stand out as being the kind to collect trophies and eventually kill someone they're obsessing over?"

Lonnie and Lacy both said they'd be very surprised to find that any of the eight male students or nine male staff members were the person we were looking for. They suggested we take the list to Velma. Before she opened the diner, she'd worked as a lunch lady at the high school. While she would have left before this class graduated, she would know the staff, and would likely have heard things Lonnie and Lacy hadn't about the students. She might also have a handle on the eight students and two staff whose status they were unsure about.

"Colt told me the boxes you found were from a school project. Some kind of time capsule."

"That's right. He was going to find out if any other boxes were missing from the school."

"There aren't," Lonnie said. "An inventory was completed, and those were the only missing boxes."

"I guess that's good. It does seem there's a strong link between the boxes and the fate of the first three girls. Did he ever find Darcy's boyfriend?"

"He did," Lonnie confirmed. "He'd had a fight with Darcy earlier in the day and taken off for a few days to calm down. He doesn't actually have an alibi because he took off alone and just drove around and stayed in cheap motel rooms for which he paid cash. I think Colt still has him as a suspect but doesn't think he's guilty."

Wilder was probably right. Adam as the killer didn't fit if all the girls with boxes were the target of the same person.

"Did he ever find the girl in the photo he was showing around? The one that was posted to social media shortly after Darcy left the bar?"

Lonnie shook his head. "Not yet. He's still looking, but so far, no one knows who she is."

"It seems like this should be easy to figure out if the same person targeted Karen, Darcy, Carrie, and Tracy," Lacy said. "How many people could there be with motive to want to do harm to all of them?"

Good question. My gut told me there was something we were missing. Something that would begin to make sense of something so senseless.

Chapter 12

Rufus apparently decided that sleeping on top of the covers was no longer good enough for him and had begun snuggling under the covers and curling up against my back. He was warm and provided a certain amount of comfort, so I didn't mind as much as I would have thought I would just a short time ago, but now I was positioning myself to accommodate his needs, which, when I examined the fact that I was afraid to move at night, was kind of ridiculous.

I rolled over, pulled up the sheet, and looked under the mountain of blankets on the bed. "Good morning, handsome. It's time to get up."

Rufus yawned.

"I know you like to snuggle up under the covers, but I have a crick in my neck from staying in one position all night. I think we may need to work out a different system than this one, where you sleep wherever you want and I sleep around you."

"Meow."

"Yes, it does smell like Georgia is up and has made coffee. Let's get up before she starts breakfast. I was thinking we'd head over to Velma's."

"Meow."

"If the place isn't crowded, I'm sure she'll make you eggs."

I flung the covers off and crawled out of my warm bed into the cold room. I used the remote to turn up the heat, then padded into the bathroom.

******

Velma had been standing behind the counter, chatting with the only two customers, when we walked in. Now she said, "Morning, girls. How was your weekend?"

We sat down at a nearby table. "It was really nice. I had dinner with Lonnie and Lacy and their six children last night. Six seems like so many, but they make it feel just right."

"I know the triplets came as quite a shock, but they were able to roll with the punches and built the sort of family most of us only dream of. Can I get you some coffee?"

We both nodded.

"How's the remodel coming?" Velma asked as she handed us menus.

"The demolition crew showed up in full force today. It's both loud and dusty, but I'm excited to see the house begin to come together. With so many workers in the place all at once, life is about to get pretty hectic."

"Which is why we ducked out and came here for breakfast." Georgia laughed.

Velma turned toward the two women at the counter. "Abby here bought the house on the bluff. She's going to fix it up and open it as an inn, which Georgia will run."

"Charlee Weaver," a tall, thin woman with white hair pulled back in a bun and faded blue eyes introduced herself. "And this is Wanda Rigby."

"Great to meet you both." I smiled in return.

"I'm happy to hear someone's going to fix up that old house," said Wanda, a woman with short brown hair streaked with gray. "It's been sitting empty as long as I can remember."

"I always have thought it would make a lovely inn," Charlee added. "The view from the house must be spectacular."

"It is pretty nice," I agreed.

"Are the kids in the car?" Velma asked, after topping off Charlee and Wanda's mugs from the coffeepot.

"They are," Georgia answered.

"Well, bring them on in. I'll give them some breakfast in the mudroom. Are the two of you ready to order?"

"I'll just have the special," I said.

Georgia seconded that, then went out to get the animals.

"Abby here is a writer," Velma informed Charlee and Wanda. "Mysteries and whatnot."

"What have you written?" Wanda asked.

I named a few of my titles.

"You're Abagail Sullivan?"

I nodded.

"I've read several of your books. I really enjoy your women's fiction. Please don't tell me you're going to stop writing now that you're opening an inn."

"No, I'm not quitting. I'll be writing while Georgia runs the inn. Do the two of you live here in Holiday Bay?"

"For over forty years," Charlee answered.

"Charlee is a retired history teacher," Velma supplied. "She taught at the high school for over thirty years. And Wanda was the school nurse for more than twenty years until she retired two years ago."

"So you both must have known Darcy Jared," I said as Georgia returned with the animals.

"Abby found boxes in the basement of her house that may solve Darcy's murder," Velma explained.

"What sort of boxes?" Charlee asked.

I told them what I'd found and what I believed they could indicate. "Lonnie and Lacy Parker and I looked at yearbook photos of the students and staff from the year the four girls were seniors and came up with twenty-two students and twelve staff who still live around here. Now that I think about it, both of your names are on that list. I'm not accusing anyone of anything. It was just the next step, because the boxes were from the time capsule project."

"Do you have that list with you?" Charlee asked.

I opened my purse and pulled it out.

She held out her hand and I gave it to her. "The eight students and two staff on the bottom of the list are people the Parkers weren't sure still lived in this area but couldn't say for sure."

"So you think one of the people on this list killed Darcy?" Wanda asked.

"I don't know anything for certain, and as I said, I'm not making accusations. The four boxes were part of a senior high school project. Three of the four girls whose time capsules ended up in my basement are either missing or dead. It can't hurt to explore that link."

After a bit of further discussion, we determined that of the people Lonnie and Lacy were unsure of, three of the students were still in town. That left a total of thirty-seven people, twenty-five students—eleven male and fourteen female—and twelve staff—seven male and five female—all of whom still lived here.

Velma frowned as she looked at the list. "I understand your reasoning, but I can't believe anyone on this list would harm those girls. There has to be another explanation."

"And there may very well be," I assured Velma. "This is just a theory. And it isn't even grounded in anything more than a hunch."

"Have you talked to Colt about this?" Velma asked.

"No. Not really. I haven't spoken to him since the day I showed him the boxes."

"Is it your theory that the person who killed Darcy has been a friend to all four girls since high school?" Wanda asked.

"Not necessarily. He or she may not have been friends with any of the four girls in high school. I do think they might be part of their circle of influence. Someone who was around but may not have been good friends with any of them. The person we're looking for could have been a student or a teacher."

Charlee sat back and crossed her arms. "I taught at the high school for more than thirty years, so this is hitting close to home. I'm finding myself mentally reviewing every staff member and every student on the list and being revolted by the thought that any one of them could be a killer."

"I agree," Wanda said. "I understand why someone who's new to town and doesn't know the people involved might come to the conclusion you have, but I don't think you'll find Darcy's killer on this list. Besides, you think Darcy, Karen, and Carrie might all be victims of the same killer. From what I heard, Carrie took off of her own free will."

"She didn't take off," Velma said with conviction. "There's a lot about this I'm unsure of, but the one thing I know is that that girl didn't desert her baby." Velma took a deep breath, obviously struggling with her emotions. After a moment, she looked at Georgia and me and continued. "Carrie had a tough life. She was brought up by an aunt when her mom died and her dad was sent to prison. She worked hard and did well in school. She worked for me in the summer and part time during the year. It was important to her to pay her own way. When she found out she was pregnant, she told the father, who immediately told her he wasn't interested in her baby. Carrie didn't panic as many young women in her situation would have; she hunkered down and did what it took to raise that baby on her own. She got a full-time job as a cashier at the market and volunteered at the day care center in exchange for babysitting. She never stopped attending church and had been dating Grayson Porter. Life always had been hard on her, but she was a fighter, a survivor. There's no way in hell she'd throw in the towel and abandon everything she'd worked so hard for, and she would never have deserted that baby."

"Were there any suspects in her disappearance?" I asked.

"The detective spoke to Grayson and a few of her friends, but when there wasn't a record of the call she supposedly received from her friend, he was sure she ran away," Charlee said.

"What happened to the baby?" I asked.

"She's living with Carrie's aunt," Velma answered.

"Did Grayson Porter go to the local high school?" I asked.

"No," Wanda said. "He moved to town shortly before he started dating Carrie."

Which probably meant he wasn't a suspect unless my theory was totally wrong and the girls' deaths weren't related to the boxes in the basement or each other. "Other than Grayson and the baby, who did she hang out with?"

No one spoke.

"She must have had friends," I encouraged.

"She was awfully busy," Velma said. "Between the baby, her job, and her volunteer work, she didn't have time for socializing."

"I understand how a woman who writes mysteries and spends her time thinking up murder plots might become interested in the fate of girls whose belongings she found in the house she recently purchased," Wanda said, "but I'm not sure there's a single person responsible for everything. Karen Stinson died from a fall, didn't she?"

"Maybe," I acknowledged. "From what I've been told, Karen liked to hike and ski. It makes sense she could have been out hiking and taken a fall. I understand she was a bit of a loner and would have been hiking alone. But Lacy told me her kids attended the preschool where Karen taught, and she frequently spoke to the kids about wilderness safety. It seems she would have been careful when out on her own." A thought occurred to me. "Is the preschool where Karen worked also the day care center where Carrie volunteered?"

"Yes, it's the same," Velma answered. "This is a small town. The place has day care for children from six months to five years and a preschool for those three to five."

"I know Darcy was single and worked in a bar, but just out of curiosity, did she have any connection to that facility?"

"She picked up her niece and nephew most afternoons," Wanda supplied. "Her sister Michelle has four children who all need transportation to or from one thing or another most days, so Darcy helped out when she could."

I frowned. I'd linked three of the four girls to the day care center. Should I try for a perfect four? "What about Tracy Edwards?" I asked. She was also single and had only recently returned to town after moving away after high school. "Did she have any connection to the preschool?"

All three women said she most likely didn't.

Too bad; I'd been on a roll with that one for a minute.

******

After we returned to the cottage, I went to the main house to check on the demolition crew's progress. Talk about a loud and dusty chaos. Lonnie had requested three dumpsters to be delivered from the refuse company and two of them were already full.

"Wow! It looks so different in here."

Lonnie was standing in the kitchen, which was now empty of cabinets and appliances. "Once we get those old doors out, it's really going to open up the space. Have you decided on materials for the cabinets and countertops?"

"I have it narrowed down to a few options. I'll take another look at the samples and let you know so you can get everything ordered."

"If you don't like any of the samples I picked out for you, there are more. A lot more, in fact. If you want to see something specific, just let me know."

"Thanks. It helps to look at an actual piece of wood rather than just photos of cabinets. As for the countertops, I'm thinking granite. I'd love to get a peek at some slabs so I can get a feel for how the grain runs throughout."

"I know a guy who has slabs. He has a warehouse in Portland. I'll arrange for you to visit if you'd like."

"Thanks. I might do that. For now, I'll take another look at the samples and try to narrow things down." I walked to the back, where they were dismantling a bathroom to build the walk-in pantry. "The suite we're building for Georgia will go on the other side of this wall?"

"Right. I'm going to tap into the old plumbing for her bathroom. I'll upgrade everything, of course, but the line to the main should be fine. As long as you're here, let me ask what you want us to do with the stuff in the attic."

"Do you need to do something with it right now?"

"No. The crew here can carry it down if you want to toss it, but it can stay where it is if you want to take your time. My plan is to demolish the whole place at once, then rebuild it one room at a time when I have my skilled laborers and subcontractors here."

"So this team is just here for the teardown?"

"Pretty much. My journeymen are finishing up another job, but they should be ready to start once the grunt work is done."

"I think I'd like to leave the stuff in the attic alone until I have time to look through it. You never know when a treasure might be lurking in an old box marked dishes."

Lonnie laughed. "I like the way you think. We'll do the teardown for the first three floors but leave the attic and basement untouched for the time being."

I nodded. "Great. By the way, I wanted to thank you again for dinner last night. You have a beautiful family."

"They are pretty great. And Lacy was thrilled you wanted to spend time with us after your first visit. She's already bugging me about having you and Georgia over soon."

"We'd enjoy that. I'd invite you to my cottage, but I'm not sure you'd all fit."

"Maybe when this grand lady is done, we can all have dinner in your fabulous new dining room on the awesome table Lacy is refinishing for you."

"Count on it."

I returned to the cottage and got out the samples Lonnie had given me, beginning to look through them again. For the cabinets, I wanted something with a country look and feel. White? Perhaps. Or maybe a blue stain on darker wood? Or even gray? I should ask Georgia for her input. Ultimately it was my decision, but I'd noticed she had a good eye when it came to visualizing the way different colors and materials worked together.

"What's with the frown?" Georgia asked when she came in from walking Ramos.

"I'm trying to pick materials for the kitchen. I know I want granite for the countertops, hardwood cabinets, and hardwood floors, but trying to decide what sort of wood to use for the floor and cabinets and what color granite to use for the countertops is proving to be more difficult than I thought it would be."

"Are you thinking of going with light or dark granite?"

"I'm not sure. I guess it depends on whether the cabinets are light or dark."

Georgia sat down next to me. "It's hard to get a feel from these small samples."

"Lonnie knows of a place in Portland where I can look at slabs. Do you want to take a drive?"

"Sure. I'm up for it."

******

Later, when Georgia and I returned to the cottage, we turned on the gas fireplace and got into our pajamas. She snuggled on the sofa with Ramos and I snuggled in the big lounge chair with Rufus. It had been a successful day. I chose a dark gray granite with streaks of black for the countertops, with cabinets stained with a light gray finish. The floor would be a deep, rich walnut, the appliances stainless steel. I'd decided to go with glass-faced cabinets that would display the white plates and cobalt-blue serving pieces. Georgia helped me draw it out, and I felt the colors we'd chosen captured the country inn aspect as well as the feel of the sea.

On the way back from Portland, we'd stopped at Lonnie and Lacy's house so I could introduce Lacy to Georgia. As predicted, the two hit it off, and by the time we left, it almost seemed we'd all known one another for years. Lacy invited us to the football buffet she'd planned for a week from Sunday. There would be other friends at the gathering, and Georgia and I figured it would provide an opportunity for us to meet others in the community.

"It was nice of you to offer to bring food for the football game," I said as Georgia poured over a binder, looking for appropriate recipes.

"I love to cook and I've been working on new recipes for the inn. I'm thrilled to have a room full of victims to try my new inventions on."

"Victims?" I chuckled.

Georgia smiled. "Until proven otherwise."

"You seem to be enjoying the challenge of finding the perfect football food. Did you entertain a lot before..." I hesitated, "well, before everything?"

"My husband and I entertained frequently. I had a nice house with a lot of room I was proud to show off. Much of it was business-related. My husband invited clients over for drinks or dinner. I had quite a few friends from work and the gym I belonged to, and, of course, we had neighbors we spent time with, as well as friends from college."

"Do you stay in touch with any of them?"

Georgia frowned. "No. I might reach out to a few people one day. I suppose some of them would have stood by me during the hell that preceded my husband's suicide. It was my choice to shut them out. Initially, I was embarrassed that the man who'd ruined so many lives was the person I'd chosen to spend mine with. And then, after Jeff killed himself, I just wanted to get as far away from my old life as I could. Everything was such a mess. I'd had this perfect life. At least, I thought I had. And then, in the blink of an eye, it was gone. I'd felt cheated that everything had been stripped away from me, and then I'd think about the lives of those Jeff had stolen from and how they must feel cheated as well, and I'd feel guilty and ashamed. I didn't steal their life savings and I had no knowledge of what he was doing, but I still felt responsible. It was all too much."

"Do you think you'll ever go back?"

Georgia looked me in the eye. "Never. How about you? Do you think you'll ever go back to San Francisco?"

I thought about the friends I still had there. I thought about the expressions of pity in their eyes, and the diverted glances and soft whispers that accompanied my entering a room. "No, I don't think so. I'm not ready to say never, but this place suits me for now. I see no reason to leave." I got up and refilled my teacup. "I'll need to get back to work, though, or staying here won't be an option."

Georgia leaned back and adjusted her position to allow her giant dog more room. "Speaking of work, how's the book going? I know you've been working on it, but you haven't talked about it."

"Slowly. I need a hook. I have a bunch of ideas, but they peter out once I start typing. I need something with meat."

Georgia scratched Ramos behind the ears. "The story of these four girls seems to have meat. Maybe you can adapt it to fiction."

I raised a brow. "I like that idea. There are a lot of elements at play. I'd like to wait until the real investigation is wrapped up, but maybe, after all the i's are dotted and t's crossed." I took a sip of my tea. "Do you want to spend some time decorating tomorrow? I've been envying Lacy's decorations and wanting to bring some Christmas cheer to this place."

"I'd love to. I saw the most awesome garland in town. It would look perfect on the mantel with a few candles and some red bows."

I settled back with Rufus and listened to Georgia as she rambled on. I'd never really had a close girlfriend. Not one with whom I lived and shared quiet evenings making plans. I missed Ben and Johnathan more than I could ever say, but in these quiet moments, when things didn't seem quite as overwhelming, I found the part of myself where hope and happiness and joy still lived though I'd thought it might have died forever with them, suddenly brimming with new life.

Chapter 13

By the time Thanksgiving rolled around, the cottage was decorated with the exception of the tree we wanted to cut down ourselves once Christmas got a little bit closer, the story Georgia had suggested I might want to write was underway, and I was absolutely no closer to solving the mystery I was still pursuing. I'd gone over it again and again in my head, but the truth of the matter was, without having known the girls, I didn't know where to go. Ben had solved many cases when he hadn't known any of the victims or suspects. He had clues provided by witnesses and physical evidence, but then, he was a trained detective. I was just a curious writer.

"What do I smell?" I asked as I wandered into the kitchen from my bedroom/office, where I'd been making a few notes for the book.

"Sticky buns. I know we already have a ton of food planned, but my mom always made sticky buns for Thanksgiving breakfast when I was a kid, so I made them every year too."

I poured a cup of coffee, then slid onto a barstool. "They smell fabulous." I let the warmth from the fire melt into me as I enjoyed the little white lights Georgia and I had strung around the cottage. Christmas jazz played softly on the stereo, and combined with the decorations and the flurries outside the window, the spirit of the season was seeping into my healing heart. Rufus wandered over and began to weave his way between my legs. I reached down and picked him up. He purred as I scratched him under the chin. I was still surprised at how much this cat I'd never wanted had added to the quality of my life.

"Once the sticky buns are done, we can put the turkey in the oven and take a break while we eat them. I think the Macy's Thanksgiving Day Parade will be on soon."

"You mentioned your mother. Do you have family somewhere who are missing you today?" I asked.

Georgia shook her head. "I'm an only child and my parents have both passed away. I have grandparents I exchange cards with, but I think my presence reminds them that their child died much too young, so they don't encourage me to visit over the holidays."

"Your parents were in an accident?"

"Plane crash when I was nineteen. They were on vacation with friends and got caught in a storm."

"I'm so sorry."

Georgia shrugged. "It was a long time ago and I found a way to get past it. How about you? Any parents or siblings?"

I paused. "My father left my mother when I was five and my mother died of cancer when I was twenty-two. I do have a sister. Annie."

"Are you close?"

I glanced out at the sea in the distance as I took a sip of my coffee. "We were. After Ben and the baby died, I was so lost. Annie tried to be there for me. She tried to help me work through my grief. But I wasn't ready to do that. If anything, I wrapped myself up in it as if that somehow would help me to make sense of everything. Annie did what she could, but I pushed her away."

"I'm sure she understood why you did it."

"Maybe. But she didn't understand why I took half of the inheritance Annie and I received from our grandmother to pay cash for this house. When I told her what I planned, she thought I'd lost my mind. She tried to talk me out of my decision, and when I wouldn't listen, she hired an attorney and tried to stop me legally."

"Stop you legally? Did she have some sort of power of attorney?"

"No. She argued that I wasn't in my right mind, was unable to make good decisions regarding my finances. She didn't have a case, of course, and I bought the house, but she hasn't spoken to me since."

"Oh Abby. I'm so sorry. How awful for you."

I took a deep breath. "I love Annie and I want to have her in my life, but I knew I needed this. I needed something. I couldn't rebuild my life in California, where everything reminded me of what I'd lost."

"Totally understandable. Maybe with time she'll be able to see things differently."

"Maybe. I've been emailing her since I got here. Short, chatty emails about the house and Holiday Bay. I can see she's opening them, but she hasn't responded. Maybe she will. In time."

Georgia placed a hand on my arm. "I'm sure she will."

"I wonder if we should build some sort of seating area along the bluff, where we can serve our guests afternoon tea, or maybe we can do wine tastings."

Georgia didn't bat an eye at the abrupt change of subject. I imagine we both were happy to move on to a topic a bit less emotional than our lack of family connections.

"Maybe a gazebo," she answered. "There aren't any trees to provide shade once you get away from the house."

"A gazebo would work," I agreed. "We'd need to find a place that didn't interfere with the view from the main house or the cottage."

"We can take a walk later to take a look. I bet Lonnie will have some ideas as well. You know, if there was a gazebo perched on the bluff, we could consider hosting weddings."

I nodded. "I like that idea. It's a gorgeous view. We could provide a full-service experience. The wedding could take place in the gazebo, but we could host the reception in the main house. We could rent out the four guest rooms to the wedding party or out-of-town guests. Definitely something to think about."

"It occurred to me we could do theme weekends too. Murder mystery weekends, English tea parties, old-fashioned Victorian Christmases. Of course, something like that might work better if we had a few additional rooms."

"Maybe, for the short term at least, you should continue staying with me here. We could use the downstairs suite as a fifth rental, and I might talk to Lonnie about converting the attic into another suite as well."

Georgia hesitated. "Six suites to rent out would be better if we decided to do theme weekends, but are you sure it won't be too invasive having Rufus and me here on a more permanent basis?"

I shrugged. "I think it will be fine for a while. We can always reclaim the downstairs suite as a manager's suite if need be. Or we can build a second little cottage. There's a lot of land here, so there's plenty of space to spread out."

Georgia grinned. "I do love the idea of theme weekends. Given the name, Inn at Holiday Bay, I can see us doing a different theme weekend for every holiday."

"Let's start a file with ideas," I suggested. "We can begin compiling supply lists and marketing plans. Then, when the house is ready, we can jump right in."

Georgia laughed. "I've noticed you like lists."

"Lists are a tangible way for me to organize my thoughts. Without them, I have a ton of ideas but no follow-through."

"I'll grab my iPad and we can open a new file," Georgia offered. "I have a ton of thoughts already."

Georgia and I bounced ideas off each other as we watched the parade. The more we talked, the more things seemed to flow. Georgia was good with graphics programs that allowed us to convert a lot of our thoughts into actual designs. The longer we talked, the more enthusiastic I became.

******

We walked Ramos along the snow-covered bluff when the parade was over and we'd gotten the turkey in the oven. I let the quiet of the moment sooth my mind as I tilted my face to the sky. There were a few flurries in the air. Not enough to be a problem, but enough to provide atmosphere. I didn't plan on launching into a mushy speech, but somehow there it was. "I want to thank you for everything." I paused. "For being here, for making dinner, and for coming up with so many innovative ideas for the inn. I want to thank you for being the friend I didn't realize I needed and for putting up with my unpredictable highs and lows. I want to thank you for making my life tolerable again."

"Oh Abby." Georgia stopped walking and hugged me. "It's me and Ramos who should be thanking you. You gave us a home, you gave us hope, and you gave us a new beginning. We can never repay you for that."

"You already have."

I let the conversation pause as we continued to walk along the path that hugged the bluff and overlooked the sea. It was a quiet day. Calm. Peaceful. It felt like a day for remembering the past and then letting it go. "It happened the week before Thanksgiving," I said in a soft voice after a while. "The accident," I clarified. I continued to walk as the memories played in my mind. "I was sitting at the table making a list of everything I needed to accomplish when there was a knock on the door. I'm not sure how I knew, but I did even before I answered." I let my thought dangle there for an instant before I continued. "It was such a shock. So very abrupt. I felt as if a train had slammed into me and left me broken and battered." I paused again and looked out at the sea. "I guess in a way that's exactly what happened. I didn't know what to do, what to say, how to feel. I do remember not wanting to go on, wanting to be dead so I could be with Ben and Johnathan."

I appreciated that Georgia listened but didn't speak. Most people I'd tried to talk to about my feelings after the accident had grown uncomfortable and tried to fill the empty space with chatter, but Georgia knew just what to do. "I'm not sure how I got through those first months, but somehow I did. Over time, the pain began to ease just a bit, and I began to feel as if I could actually breathe. It was a long road, but at some point I realized I wanted to live. I had things I still wanted to do with my life. Last summer wasn't too bad, but then, as fall approached, I began to have panic attacks. I knew I needed a change, so I bought the house on a whim. Paid cash so the escrow only took a couple of weeks. I've spent more time picking out shoes than I did giving up my life in California and moving to Maine."

Georgia wound her fingers through mine as we continued to walk. She squeezed my hand, and I knew she was there with me. Two wounded birds trying to build a new nest after the old one was destroyed.

"Of course, once I got here and saw exactly what I had gotten myself in to, I began to panic again."

Georgia smiled.

"And then I met Lonnie, and somehow he made the impossible feel possible. I went from running away from something to wanting to build something. I've really been dreading the holidays, but now that I have you and Ramos and Lonnie and Lacy and this big-ass house and let's not forget my big-ass cat, I feel something akin to happiness. Yes, it's tinged with sadness, but I know I can and will survive. So thank you for that."

Georgia stopped walking and hugged me again. It was a long, hard hug that let me know she was really there for me. When I'd purchased the house on the bluff I wasn't sure exactly what I would find, but in that moment I knew I had found exactly what I needed.

Chapter 14

The Holiday Bay Christmas Festival was in full swing and the town was packed with tourists looking for a hometown Christmas experience. Georgia and I had decided to embrace the charm of the small seaside town we had both committed to calling home. The main street was lined with cute mom-and-pop shops on both sides of the street. In front of the row of shops was a wide sidewalk that was lined with bright red streetlamps wrapped with white ribbon to present the appearance of candy canes. Between each streetlamp were two patio trees, currently strung with small white lights that gave the entire village a holiday feel despite the moody skies and snow flurries in the air.

Street vendors were out en masse selling everything from turkey legs to hot cider to chestnuts roasted over an open fire. Carolers, dressed in Victorian garb, cruised the streets, their voices raised as they serenaded the visitors who had brought their holiday money to the tiny community. I walked with a slight hop to my step as we strolled through perfectly decorated shops, each playing carols and offering unique gifts for the discriminating holiday shopper.

"Abby, Georgia," Charlee greeted us when we stepped into Mary Christmas's sweet shop. "How are you enjoying your first Christmas Festival?"

"Very much. It's obvious everyone is really committed. The town looks wonderful."

"This festival is our biggest fund-raiser of the year. The merchants know it and do whatever it takes to bring in the tourist dollar." Charlee turned to the man to her left, who appeared to be in his mid or late thirties. "Have you met my nephew, Tanner Peyton?"

We shook our heads, so she performed the introductions. "Abby and Georgia are turning the old house on the bluff into an inn," she added.

"Then we're neighbors," Tanner said. "I own the property to the south of yours."

"I saw it when I had to take a detour when the road was closed. You own a ranch?" I asked.

"Actually, it's a kennel. Peyton Academy. I train service dogs."

"Like police dogs?" asked Georgia, whose blue eyes lit up whenever dogs were mentioned.

"Search-and-rescue dogs. I provide animals for local groups as well as FEMA."

"Wow," Georgia gushed. "That must be so rewarding."

I noticed Tanner seemed drawn to the blond-haired pixie who seemed to be hanging on his every word. "It is. You should come by sometime and I'll give you a tour."

"Thank you. I'd like that very much."

"Georgia has a big Newfoundland named Ramos," I offered. "He doesn't have any special skills other than allowing himself to be bossed around by my giant cat, but we think he's pretty special. Why don't you come by the house sometime? Georgia and I can give you our tour and share our plans for the inn with you. While you're there, you can meet Ramos."

"I'd enjoy that."

"Georgia can give you her number. You can text her before you come, to be sure we're around."

We chatted with Charlee and Tanner for a few more minutes, then continued on our way.

"What was that all about?" Georgia asked.

"What was what all about?"

"You practically shoved my phone number down that poor man's throat."

I grinned at her as she protested just a bit too much. "I saw the way you were practically drooling over him."

"I wasn't drooling over him; I was drooling over the dogs he said he trains. I love dogs. You know that."

I shrugged. "Maybe. But you have to admit he's a babe. All that thick black hair, that crooked smile, and those baby blue eyes that seem to look straight into your soul."

Georgia laughed. "Sounds like you're the one who's drooling."

"Perhaps. In another lifetime. But I'm not in the market for a guy, whether he's a babe or not."

"Trust me, neither am I."

"Okay. So we'll show him around and then we'll go look at his place and that'll be that."

Georgia nodded. "Okay. It does seem like getting to know our closest neighbor would be the right thing to do. I mean, you never know when we might have an emergency."

"Or need to borrow a cup of sugar," I added.

Georgia giggled. "Now you're just being silly. But as long as you've brought up the subject of sugar, we do need some. With all the baking I've been doing, we're going through quite a lot."

"I've seen you baking, but I haven't noticed that many cookies or cakes around."

"I volunteered to help out with the bake sale in town. It's for a good cause, and I made sure that all the cakes, cookies, and pies I donated were wrapped in plastic with the Inn at Holiday Bay logo we designed the other night across the front. There's even a teaser about a grand opening when the renovations are complete."

I looped my arm through Georgia's. "You're a marketing genius."

"I like to be helpful, and I want our enterprise to be a success. I know it's early, but we might want to establish a phone number people can call to get information and a website with photos of the renovation and teasers about upcoming events. I think it will serve us well to build up the hype so that when we open, we have folks standing in line to rent our very lovely, very expensive rooms."

"I love both of those ideas." I paused at the chestnut stand and purchased a bag.

"Great. If you want to handle the phone line, I'll set up the web page. Once I have the basic page built, we can work together on the design. We'll want to have business cards soon too. It's never too soon to get the word out."

We chatted about the inn and the empire Georgia was planning to build, ate junk food, listened to carols, and had a wonderful time.

"My feet are starting to hurt from all this walking," I said. "Let's stop by Velma's for something to eat."

"Sounds good to me. I could use a break," Georgia answered.

We turned around and walked back the way we'd come. When we entered the diner, we found what could only be described as chaos. "Wow, it's packed in here," Georgia commented.

"Yes. Maybe this wasn't a good idea."

Georgia looked around. "It looks like Velma is alone. I'm going to see if I can help."

I watched as Georgia wove her way through the crowd. She said something to Velma, who nodded, then hugged her. Georgia pointed to me and Velma waved. Then she said something else to Velma and made her way back to me.

"One of Velma's waitresses called in sick. I'm going to stay to help for a while."

"Is there anything I can do?" I asked.

"Well, if you want to help Velma out here, I can pitch in in the kitchen."

"I've never waited tables before."

"Just write down what they want. If the order seems too complicated, grab Velma. I bet most of these folks are just here for a sandwich and coffee."

"Okay. I'll do what I can."

Two hours later, the lunch crowd had cleared out and the place was close to empty. Velma closed at two and it was already after that, so there wouldn't be any new customers wandering in. I took a stool at the counter. Now my feet were really throbbing.

"Thank you so much," Velma said. "Both of you. I don't know what I would have done if you hadn't come in."

"No problem. I messed up a few orders, but I did better than I thought I would. Being a waitress is hard."

"I had fun," Georgia said, joining them at the counter. "I forgot what a rush it is to juggle ten orders at a time."

"Any time you get bored, feel free to come on down and cook for a spell." Velma chuckled.

"I might take you up on that." Georgia grinned. "There's a takeout order that was never picked up. It's a cold one: a roast beef sandwich and potato salad."

"It's for Colt. I told him I'd have someone drop it off at his office."

"I'll take it," I said.

"And I'll help you clean up," Georgia offered.

"Oh, you don't have to do that," Velma said.

Georgia slipped off her stool. "I don't mind. Abby can deliver Chief Wilder's lunch, and by the time she's back, we should have the kitchen tidied up."

Velma, who looked both exhausted and appreciative, nodded.

I grabbed the sack lunch and walked down the busy street. The crowd created an atmosphere that was both stimulating and exhausting. The street vendors planned to sell their wares until dark and the shops were open late on the weekends. It would be fun to come back after dark sometime, when the lights would really be lovely.

"Chief Wilder," I greeted him as I walked in through the front door of the police station.

"Ms. Sullivan," he responded from the desk behind the reception counter. It appeared he was the only one in the station today.

I held up the sack. "I brought your lunch from Velma's. She was shorthanded today, so Georgia and I are helping out.

Wilder smiled and stood up. "That's very nice of you."

"Are you alone today?" I asked.

"The receptionist called in sick. Something must be going around."

"It seems so. Velma's waitress called in sick too." I looked around the station. There was a small Christmas tree in the corner, and someone had strung white lights around all the windows. "I like the decorations. Very homey."

"Peach can be credited with them." Wilder opened the brown paper bag and peeked inside.

"Any news on Darcy's murder investigation?" I asked as casually as I could.

"I do have some news, actually. A man named Bronson Vender was arrested just this morning."

I frowned. "Bronson Vender?" The name didn't sound familiar. I was sure his wasn't one of the names on the high school list.

"Mr. Vender is the man you told me about in Velma's that day; the one from the bar who was ogling Darcy. I tracked him down at the lodge up north. Initially, he claimed he left the bar with his friends and never saw Darcy again. I had no proof otherwise, so I had to take his word for it. Then, yesterday, I got a tip from one of the other men in his group, who said Vender let it slip he'd run into Darcy at a party after she got off shift. He told his friend he'd been drunk and not thinking clearly, and when the opportunity arose, he shoved her into his car and raped and strangled her."

I frowned. "Are you sure he killed Darcy?"

Wilder turned and set the brown bag on his desk. "I wasn't at first, but I am now. The Bangor police picked him up and he confessed to killing Darcy and dumping her in the woods."

Color me confused. "So what does that have to do with the boxes in my basement?"

"Not a darn thing."

"But there has to be a link. It would be too weird if there wasn't."

Wilder shrugged. "Odd coincidences do sometimes occur. I don't know why the time capsules of four women were stashed in your basement or who put them there, but it seems they aren't connected to anything else that's happened. Now that Vender has confessed, I'm operating on the assumption Karen really did fall to her death and Carrie really did run away. I've called Tracy Edwards to let her know it's safe to come back whenever she'd like."

"Something feels wrong about this," I said.

"Weren't you the one who told me about Vender in the first place?"

"Well, yes."

"And at the time, didn't you tell me you felt he made a good suspect?"

"Yes, it seemed he did."

"And he did confess to the police in Bangor when they picked him up. We also have the statement of the friend he spilled his guts to. I don't think there's any doubt he killed Darcy Jared."

"No, I guess there isn't." I glanced at the sack. "Enjoy your sandwich."

"I will, and thank you for delivering it."

I headed back through the crowds to Velma's place. I had no reason to believe Vender didn't kill Darcy. In fact, it made total sense. But if Vender really killed Darcy and Karen really slipped and fell to her death, what was up with the boxes in the basement and, more importantly, where was Carrie Long?

Chapter 15

By the time mid-December rolled around, the remodel was well underway, the mystery of the boxes in the basement had faded into the woodwork, and the novel I'd finally committed to was coming along nicely. I'd sent sample chapters to Kate and she loved it. For the first time in over a year, I felt like Abagail Sullivan, Author, was finally back, and that feeling was pretty awesome.

Georgia and I had made so many plans for the inn in the past two weeks that I began to dream about theme weekends and wine tastings. I couldn't remember the last time I'd been so excited about anything, which was amazing in and of itself. Tanner Peyton had come by for a tour of the house and property and he'd given Georgia and me a tour of his place in return. He had an impressive operation, and I could tell by those first few interactions that he was destined to be a friend, not just a neighbor.

The hoopla surrounding Darcy's death died down to nothing more than a quiet murmur after the news that her killer had been found was released. Everyone was still sorry about what had happened to her, but I think most of the town was happy to get back to their lives and enjoying the upcoming holidays without worrying about a killer on the loose. I'd let the mystery of the boxes in the basement take a back seat in my mind as well, though the fate of Carrie Long continued to haunt me. I wasn't sure why. I hadn't known her and I no longer had a reason to believe she'd met with foul play, although those who knew her best were still committed to the belief that she would never have left her baby voluntarily, and based on what I knew, I agreed with them. She was missing for almost three months by now, so if she was alive and didn't want to be found, finding her would be difficult. Still, her image popped into my head at the oddest times, almost demanding I finish what I'd started and find out what had happened to the young mother on that September night when she seemed to have disappeared off the face of the earth.

"Tanner is having an open house this evening for a group of investors and his caterer totally flaked out," Georgia informed me when I put aside my writing to take a break. "I volunteered to help out. His housekeeper went into town to pick up the things we'll need and I'm going over there now. You're welcome to come."

"I'm not a great cook so I don't know how much help I'll be, but I'll join you. Just let me shut down my computer and grab a jacket."

"I already took Ramos out and fed and watered both animals, so I'll wait for you in the car," Georgia said.

Tanner Peyton's estate was perched on the edge of the sea. Like mine, his featured a majestic house;

unlike my property, which was otherwise vacant except for the guest cottage, Tanner's place was fenced into smaller sections, each one housing a kennel and outdoor dog runs.

Like every other property in Holiday Bay, Peyton Academy was decorated in holiday splendor. The long white fence that lined the drive had been strung with colorful lights and the giant fir trees that framed the front gate had been decked out with lights as well. I looked at the trees in awe as we passed through the gate. He must have had the fire department come out with a ladder to get the lights so high in the trees.

Tanner's home was built from logs that, he'd informed us during our tour, had come from northern Maine. Unlike my home, which had multiple stories, Tanner's was spread out ranch style. The front porch was made from natural stone and led up to a hardwood door that held a colorfully lit wreath.

The place was natural and woodsy, yet elegant as well.

"Tanner said to just come in and go back to the kitchen," Georgia said.

I grabbed the box filled with spices and herbs she'd brought, while she carried a box of cookbooks and specialty pans. The housekeeper was picking up the basic supplies, but Georgia explained, there were some things she wouldn't be able to get at the small market that served Holiday Bay.

While I was excited about my own house, which would feature painted walls, wainscoting, and crown molding for a country feel, Tanner's natural log walls were lovely as well.

When we arrived in the gourmet kitchen, Tanner was talking to a young woman with blond hair and blue eyes who looked young enough to be his daughter.

"Oh good, you made it." Tanner smiled at Georgia and took the box from her hands.

It was obvious Tanner had eyes only for Georgia, so I set my box on the counter and smiled at the woman Tanner had been chatting with.

Tanner introduced us. "Georgia Carter, Abby Sullivan, this is my sister, Nikki Peyton."

"Pleased to meet you both," Nikki said with a smile. "The way Tanner has been going on and on about y'all, I've been curious to get a peek at you."

"On and on?" I said. "Really?"

Tanner glared at Nikki. "Nikki is my half sister. She likes to tease, but if she isn't careful, she's going to find herself back in Texas."

"Texas?" I asked.

"Tanner and I share a father but have different mothers," Nikki explained. "My mother divorced our father when I was six and moved us both to Texas."

"So you're visiting?" Georgia asked.

"For now, although I'm hoping Tanner will let me stay." Nikki shot him the biggest puppy dog eyes I thought I'd ever seen.

Oh yeah. She was good.

"I'm going to run over to the kennel to check on the new arrivals. I'll be back in an hour. Maria will be back with the groceries shortly. If you have any problems or any questions, you can text me." Tanner looked directly at Nikki. "Behave."

Nikki put her hands on her hips. "Don't I always?"

Tanner rolled his eyes and walked out the back door.

I turned my attention to Nikki. "You and your brother are close?" I hadn't meant it to come out as a question, but the status of their relationship did seem somewhat undefined.

Nikki shrugged. "Not really. I suppose we are now, but we weren't always. Tanner was sixteen when I was born. He lived with his mother and I lived with my mother and our father. He went off to college when I was two. By the time he graduated, my mother had divorced our father and moved us to East Texas. I don't remember even meeting Tanner until I was fifteen and my mother remarried. Her new husband and I didn't get along, so she shipped me off to live with my father, a man I barely knew. Tanner was living in California then, but he did come to visit, so we got to know each other."

"Tanner lived in California?" Georgia asked.

"For a while. He built a software company he eventually sold for millions. Maybe hundreds of millions."

"He hadn't mentioned that," I said. "If he's a software developer, how did he get into dog training?"

Nikki picked up an apple from a bowl and took a bite. She chewed it up before answering. "Tanner always loved dogs, but the real reason he sold his company and moved back to Maine to train dogs was because of his experience being rescued. He was mountain climbing with some friends up near Yosemite and fell. He had a few broken bones but was otherwise okay, but the friends couldn't get to him because he landed on a ledge. He tried to find his own way back to his friends but ended up getting lost. He spent two nights in the forest, but eventually, the search-and-rescue team found him. Tanner said that in the moment when that beautiful Lab saved him, he knew what he wanted to do with the rest of his life. A major software firm had been bugging him to sell to them for quite some time, so when he made it back to civilization, he decided to take the offer. He sold his company, bought this land, and started training dogs. His work is totally nonprofit. Tanner doesn't need the money, so he trains the dogs and matches them with first responders free of charge. He does have some investors to help out with the hard costs, like the group he's schmoozing tonight, but there's never a cost to the first responders."

"Wow," Georgia said. "That's an amazing story."

"Tanner can be a pain in the ass sometimes, but he's a good guy. But don't tell him I said that. It will destroy the balance in our relationship."

Georgia laughed. "Your secret is safe with us."

"So you went to high school here?" I asked.

"For two years, junior and senior. After that I went to college in Dallas. I graduated last June and was living with my mother, who's now divorced from husband number two. We weren't getting along, so I asked Tanner if I could come for a visit. I've been here about two weeks. Our agreement about how long I'm welcome to stay is somewhat open, but I'm going to try to get a job here and make the stay permanent. I really do love it here."

"It's a beautiful place to live," Georgia said.

"I'm back," someone yelled from the front of the house. "A little help with the groceries, please."

Nikki, Georgia, and I followed the voice outside. The Subaru station wagon Maria had been driving was filled to the roof with grocery bags. We all pitched in to transfer the supplies into the kitchen. Once they were brought in and unpacked, Georgia took charge, assigning tasks to each of us. Nikki and I were the chopping, slicing, mixing, and stirring team, while Georgia and Maria saw to the delicate work. It took us most of the afternoon, but by the time the sun went down beyond the horizon, we had enough food to feed a small army.

"I'm going to run home and change so I can get back in time to serve the food," Maria said.

"Do you need help?" Georgia asked.

Maria hesitated. "I could use the help, but you girls have already done so much."

"It's not a problem," Georgia assured her. "I'll go home and change into a dress." She looked at me. "Do you want to help?"

"Sure. I have a little black dress I've been waiting to break in."

By the time Georgia and I had returned to the Peyton house, Nikki and Maria were already setting out the food. Tanner was dressed in black pants and a dark red dress shirt that almost exactly matched the dark red of Georgia's dress. It almost made me think they'd compared notes, but I knew they hadn't.

Someone had turned on some soft Christmas jazz, which fit the atmosphere created by the twenty-foot tree in the great room. I wondered how he'd gotten the lights and ornaments on the top. Trays filled with wine and champagne were being circulated by men and women dressed in black. Nikki whispered to me that most of the waitstaff were men and women from the local search-and-rescue team, which had been the recipient of more than one of Tanner's dogs.

By the time the food had been sampled and an obnoxious amount of alcohol consumed, I was exhausted. I could see Nikki and Maria were exhausted as well, so Nikki and I volunteered to begin cleaning up while Tanner saw to the last of his guests and Maria and Georgia saw to the last of the food.

"That was some party," I said to Nikki as I filled the sink with sudsy water.

"Tanner knows how to get what he needs. I overheard someone say they'd made a six-figure donation."

"Wow. That's awesome. And amazing."

"It's pretty expensive to train even one dog. But Tanner only hires the best trainers. He's a pretty great guy."

"Yes, he is." I agreed. "And I hope it works out for you to stay in Holiday Bay. I think you're pretty great yourself."

Nikki smiled.

"So, if you went to high school here, did you know the girl who died?" I asked. That question had been on my mind since we'd spoke earlier, but I hadn't had the chance to ask.

"Yeah, I knew Darcy. She was a year ahead of me."

"I guess you heard about the time capsule project?"

Nikki spooned leftovers into a bowl. "Sure. It was kind of a big deal at the time. Darcy was the president of the student council that year, so she was credited with the idea, even though it was totally Connie Belmont's."

"Connie Belmont?"

"She was in the same class as Darcy."

"I don't remember hearing the name."

Nikki opened the refrigerator and put in the bowl she had just filled, then started on the next one. "She moved here partway through senior year. She was fun and creative, but she never could crack through new-girl status, so she didn't have a lot of friends. She and I hung out sometimes because I was new too. That's how I know the time capsule project was hers and stupid Darcy stole it and took all the credit." Nikki blushed. "Sorry. I guess it's wrong to call a dead girl stupid."

"That's okay. I understand. Does Connie still live in the area?"

"She did until a couple of years ago. She got married and moved away, which was sort of sad, but she never really fit in, so she's probably a lot happier now."

"I guess. Do you think she'll come back when they open the time capsule?"

Nikki laughed. "No. Not after what she did."

"Did?"

"Connie was in the principal's office when the senior adviser called and gave him the combination to the lock where the time capsules were kept. He wrote it down and Connie saw what he'd written. She was mad the student council had used her idea but hadn't given her any credit, so she snuck into the school and stole the boxes of all four student council members. When the capsule's opened, they're going to be shocked to find their stuff gone."

I took in a breath. "All four. I don't suppose you mean Darcy Jared, Carrie Long, Karen Stinson, and Tracy Edwards?"

"You know them?"

"I don't know them, but I know about the boxes. I found them in my basement."

"Really? Connie said she hid them where no one would ever look, but she didn't say where. Talk about a small world."

A small world indeed. "You do know that for a while, the boxes were considered to be evidence in Darcy Jared's murder investigation?"

Nikki looked genuinely surprised. "No. I hadn't heard. Why?"

"Because of the four girls whose boxes were taken, two are dead and one is missing."

"Missing? Who's missing?"

"Carrie Long. She's been missing since September."

Nikki gasped and put a hand to her mouth. "Oh my God. I only just heard Karen had died a couple of days ago when I was in town and a guy I knew from high school mentioned how odd it was that two people from his graduating class had died within months of each other. He didn't mention Carrie. What happened to her?"

I explained as much as I could. It was obvious Nikki was both horrified and saddened. "She's been on my mind a lot. I feel like someone should be looking for her, but it doesn't seem as if anyone is."

"Carrie was always nice to me," Nikki said. "Nicer than any of the others on the student council. If you want to find her, I'll help you look. In fact, I have an idea where to start."

Chapter 16

Nikki and I got started the first thing the next morning. I'd invited her to come over to the cottage so we could chat without being overheard. Tanner had a training session, and there were people lingering in the house and the kennels. Once I explained the plan to Georgia, she wanted to help as well.

I started off by telling Nikki everything I knew about Carrie's disappearance. "Carrie was last seen late at night this past September. From what I've been told, she called a neighbor to ask her to stay with her baby because a friend had called her in a panic when their car broke down and needed to be picked up. The baby was asleep, and Carrie promised to be gone no more than thirty minutes. She never returned. No one in town has reported seeing her since. Her car, her phone, and her purse have never been found."

"Wow. I had no idea. Poor Carrie."

"There's more. Before her disappearance, Carrie withdrew almost all the money in her savings account from the bank. The bank manager asked about it at the time, and Carrie said she was helping a friend."

"Sounds like this friend might have taken the money, then killed her," Nikki said.

"Perhaps. The more I think about it, the less sense the timeline makes. On one hand, calling the neighbor in the middle of the night makes it seem as if whatever happened wasn't prearranged. I mean, if you have a baby and you know ahead of time you're going to meet someone, wouldn't you set it up to meet during the day, when you can get a sitter? On the other, Carrie took the money out of the bank a couple of days before she went missing, which makes it look as if her meet up with the friend was premeditated. But why in the middle of the night? And why did she tell the neighbor she'd received a call when there was no record of her getting one?"

Nikki nibbled the corner of her thumbnail. I could see by the state of the nail this was a nervous habit of long standing. "What if Carrie's friend did contact her that night, but not by phone?"

I looked at Nikki. "What do you mean?"

"What if the friend came by Carrie's house demanding the money that had been promised him or her? What if Carrie said she didn't have it on her? Maybe she'd left it at work or hidden it in her gym locker or left it with someone else? Maybe the person threatened either Carrie or her baby if she didn't hand over the money right then and there, so Carrie called the neighbor to sit with the baby, then went with them to get it?"

"That makes sense," I said.

"It does if this person Carrie withdrew the money for wasn't really a friend," Georgia countered.

"It could be she was being blackmailed or threatened," I said.

"How do we find out what happened after Carrie left her house?" Georgia asked.

No one seemed to have a suggestion.

Finally, Georgia said, "The person Carrie withdrew the money for must have been part of her life. We know she worked at the market and the day care center and was dating Grayson Porter. Maybe we should start there. She might have said something to someone."

"That's not a bad idea," I said. "Lacy said Carrie was under a lot of stress in the days before she disappeared. She had a full-time job at the market and helped out at the day care almost full time to pay for childcare for her daughter. Lacy thought she was at the end of her rope. But what if the stress others were picking up on was due to something other than normal, day-to-day stressors? What if there was something more going on? Maybe she mentioned it to someone."

"Where should we start?" Nikki asked.

"With Grayson Porter," I said. "If Carrie was dating him, she might very well have opened up to him about what was going on in her life."

"Unless what was bothering her was embarrassing or illegal," Nikki pointed out.

"Well, yes, I guess there's always that."

None of us knew Grayson and I had no expectation he would speak to us, but Lacy knew him, so I called her to ask if she'd set up a meeting. She agreed to call him to see how receptive he was. I thanked her and waited for a callback. In the meantime, we took a stab at approaching things from another angle.

"Carrie withdrew a lot of cash—at least a lot for her—from her savings account days before she disappeared, saying it was for a friend. We know she was struggling financially and had a baby to support, so it doesn't seem logical she would just give her savings to a friend, even if the person was desperate," I began.

"Unless she was being blackmailed or threatened," Georgia added.

"Yes," I agreed. "Carrie seemed like an upstanding citizen from what others have said, but that doesn't mean she didn't have a past. Maybe her past caught up with her." I looked at Nikki.

She shrugged. "Carrie was nicer than most of the girls in high school, but she was still one of the popular girls. She was a cheerleader and on the student council, and she was gorgeous, with half the guys in the school after her. She was a good student and liked by almost everyone. She did hang out with Darcy, who was less kind, so for me, that's a mark against her. Still, I have a feeling if she got into trouble, it was probably after high school."

"Do we know anything about the baby's father?" Georgia asked.

"Not a thing," I said. "I don't remember anyone even mentioning his name."

"Maybe we should go talk to Velma," Georgia suggested. "She has total faith Carrie didn't just take off and really wanted to help her. I bet she knows a lot more than she's already told us."

Georgia took Ramos out and then the three of us headed into town. As it had been all month long, the streets and sidewalks were crowded with holiday shoppers, but we arrived at Velma's just as she was closing, so we could talk to her without worrying about a diner full of tourists listening in on our conversation.

We explained our reason for being there, and we all settled in with cups of coffee to try to sort things out.

"I don't know what Carrie was so stressed about in the days before she went missing," Velma said. "She didn't confide in me."

"She took money out of her savings. Money she couldn't afford to just give away, yet it seemed that's what she did. Why?" I asked.

"I've thought about that," Velma said. "I can't claim to know why she did it, but in my mind, the only reason she'd give away money she desperately needed to support her baby would be to protect that baby."

"Protect the baby from what? Or who?" Georgia asked.

"What about the father?" Nikki suggested. She looked at Velma. "You said the baby's father wanted nothing to do with it when Carrie told him she was expecting, so she was raising the baby on her own. What if he changed his mind? What if he came to her and said he wanted visitation or shared custody or something?"

Velma frowned. "I don't know. Would he even have a claim?"

"Did he give up his rights legally?" I asked.

"I don't know," Velma repeated.

"Was he a local boy?" I asked.

Velma shook her head. "No. Carrie met him at some camp or retreat she attended the summer before last. She considered moving up there, but then she found out she was pregnant and moved home. I never met him, but I know his name was Derek. Derek Strong."

"Do you know where he is now?" I asked.

Velma shook her head. "Carrie never said."

"Do you know the name of the camp where Carrie met him?" I asked.

Velma tapped her fingertips on the table. "I know it was just this side of the border. It seems like it was a one-word name. Like Serenity, but that isn't it. I do think it started with an S. Solitude, Surrender? No." Velma continued to drum her fingers. "Salvation. That's it. The camp was called Salvation."

We thanked Velma, then went back to the cottage. I logged onto my computer and did a search for a camp called Salvation in northern Maine. "Oh, this can't be good," I said.

"What is it?" Nikki asked.

"Salvation is the name of a compound."

"A compound?" Georgia asked.

"It's an underground sort of thing. End-of-the-world stuff, by the look of things. If Carrie was wrapped up in something like that, I'm surprised they let her leave. From what I know of end-time cults, which isn't a lot, once you're in, you're in."

"Maybe that was what the money was for," Georgia said. "Maybe she's been paying this cult off for her freedom."

"Seems like as good an explanation as any. I'm going to call Chief Wilder. Investigating an end-times cult sounds like something someone with a gun should be doing."

I called him and explained what we'd learned, and he agreed to look in to it. I'd just hung up when Lacy called to let me know Grayson was willing to speak to us and was at the church that afternoon. The three of us decided to go there immediately to see what he knew.

******

Grayson Porter was a serious-looking young man with hollow cheeks and sunken eyes. From his outward appearance, it seemed obvious he'd been under a great deal of stress. I assumed it had to do with having his girlfriend disappear in the middle of the night. Either that, or he had something to do with it. Until I spoke to him, that was a toss-up in my mind.

I took care of the introductions, and then Grayson began to speak. "Lacy said you had some questions about Carrie. I think it's odd that folks who didn't know her are looking into her disappearance, but in the end, I just want her found, so it seems we have the same goal. How can I help?"

"We're trying to understand what happened," I began. "We know she was under a lot of stress in the days before she went missing. More than usual, according to those we've spoken to. Do you know why?"

"Not specifically. She mentioned hearing from someone from her past that she'd rather not have. I don't know if that was what was behind her somewhat odd behavior, but it seems worth telling you."

"Odd behavior?" I asked.

"In the week before she went missing, Carrie seemed paranoid. She kept looking over her shoulder, and she'd jump at every little noise. I tried to talk to her about it. I asked her repeatedly what she was afraid of. All she would say was that she was jittery, and not to mind her. She said she had some things on her mind she needed to sort out but that I shouldn't worry about it."

"Did she tell you she planned to withdraw money from her savings?" I asked.

Grayson shook his head. "I didn't know a thing about it until after she went missing and the cops came to talk to me."

"Did she ever talk about her baby's father?" I asked.

Grayson looked out a window. He seemed so lost. "Not really," he answered after a bit. "I know she met him at some camp. She said she never loved him, and when he didn't want anything to do with the baby, she was just as happy. As far as I know, she didn't maintain a relationship with him. At least other than the first time, when she explained things to me, she never brought him up." Grayson looked at me. "Do you think he's involved in this?"

"I don't know," I answered honestly. "It wouldn't be unheard of for the father of a baby to come out of the woodwork later on. Chief Wilder is following up on things; if he's involved, we'll know soon enough."

Grayson ran his hands through his hair. "I guess if the baby's father is involved, that would explain

Carrie's comment about someone from her past coming back into her life."

Yes, it would.

Chapter 17

Another week passed and we were no closer to figuring out what had happened to Carrie. Chief Wilder had managed to track down Derek Strong, who hadn't left the compound in months. I supposed other end-time radicals weren't the best alibis, but the group did seem to keep a tight leash on their members, and the video cameras they had set up all around the compound proved he couldn't have been the one to meet Carrie on the night she disappeared. There was the off chance Carrie had gone to them and was inside the compound again, but the man Wilder had spoken to said he hadn't seen her in over a year, and the chief had no basis for requesting a warrant to prove otherwise.

Georgia and I talked about our frustration over Carrie's disappearance, but we'd done everything we could think of. We both needed this holiday to help mend our hearts and souls and vowed to immerse ourselves in the Christmas spirit to the best of our abilities. The thing was, Carrie wasn't a captive waiting to be rescued. As far as we could tell, she'd either run away and didn't want to be found or she was dead.

"Do you want to go to the play tonight?" Georgia asked.

I looked up from my laptop. Georgia was in the kitchen baking, as she did quite a lot. I was pretty sure she was single-handedly stocking the bake sale booth the community was running as a fund-raiser, but I didn't mind. It was excellent publicity for the inn. "Did I hear they were doing *A Christmas Carol*?"

"They are. Nikki knows some of the cast members, so we talked about going. I think Tanner is going as well."

Normally, I wouldn't want to be a third wheel with Georgia and Tanner, but if Nikki was going... "That sounds like fun. What time were you thinking?"

"The play is at eight, but we talked about having dinner before. Maybe six?"

"Works for me. Dressy or casual?"

"Casual. I'm wearing black leggings, boots, and my long red sweater. I think Nikki plans to wear something similar."

"The two of you have really hit it off."

Georgia shrugged. "I guess. She's ten years younger than I am, but we have a lot in common. And I think she's a little bit lonely. She seems to enjoy hanging out around here, and I'm happy for the help with the baking. I wonder if I should do another batch of ginger cookies."

I laughed. "Haven't you already made fifty batches of ginger cookies?"

Georgia smiled. "I guess I have. But they're selling well, which is good for the town, and the labels I put on the front of everything I package has everyone talking about the inn. I figure it's a win-win."

"I agree. Keep up the good work." I looked back down at my laptop.

"How's the book coming?" Georgia asked.

"Really good, although that isn't what I'm working on right now."

"What are you working on?"

"That thing we promised we wouldn't obsess over."

Georgia stopped what she was doing. "It's hard to move on without a resolution one way or another. Do you have a new lead?"

"Not really. I've just been thinking about Grayson's comment about Carrie saying she'd been contacted by someone from her past. Someone she wasn't thrilled to have heard from. If her baby daddy had shown up, that would make sense, but he didn't, which made me wonder who her blast from the past really was."

Georgia stepped around the counter and sat down across from me. "Any luck in figuring that out?"

I shook my head. "No. I asked Velma and Lacy if they had any ideas. They each gave me a few names, but none seemed the sort of person who would cause a large degree of stress in Carrie's life. If she was acting paranoid, this person would need to be someone she was afraid of."

"It's going to be hard to figure this out because we never even met her."

"You're right." I closed my laptop. "I'm feeling the need for some fresh air. Do you want to come with me to take Ramos for a walk?"

"I'd love to."

******

Dinner was fantastic and the play was funny, heartwarming, and all-around adorable. I'd never been part of a small, tight-knit community before. Apparently, I'd been missing quite a lot. I was having the best time. After the play, Tanner suggested we all go for a drink. The bar he selected was classy and elegant and not at all like the Reindeer Roundup. Tanner found us a table near the Christmas tree and we placed our order. I had just taken the first sip of my wine when Chief Wilder walked in. Tanner waved to him, and when he confirmed he was off duty, Tanner pulled up another chair and asked him to join us.

"Did you just get off?" Tanner asked.

Wilder nodded. "It's been a busy day, with all the tourists in town for the Festival. Just a few more days and our peaceful little town will be quiet once again. At least until the next event comes around. Are you all in town for the Festival?"

"The play," Tanner answered.

"You should try to catch it if you haven't seen it already," Georgia said. "It was wonderful."

"I'm working double shifts until the Festival is over." Wilder looked at me. "Seems you've been busy as well. Grayson Porter told me you went to see him."

"I did. I know the mystery of the boxes in my basement has been solved, but I can't get Carrie Long off my mind."

"Yeah, that's a tough one. I thought the lead about the boyfriend might pan out."

"Grayson said Carrie became stressed after she was contacted by someone from her past. When I thought the baby daddy was the guy, that fit perfectly. Now it's back to the beginning."

"Wait," Wilder said. "Grayson said Carrie told him she'd been contacted by someone from her past?"

"That's what he said. And it was someone she wasn't happy about hearing from. Do you have an idea who it might have been?"

Wilder took a sip of his beer. "Did Grayson say when it was?"

"I think he said a week or two before she went missing. You know something?"

Wilder took another sip.

"You may as well tell her," Nikki said. "She isn't going to let this go." She looked around the table. "None of us will. Not until Carrie's found one way or the other."

"Carrie's father was released from prison a month before she went missing. I didn't know that until today, and I only know it now because I decided to check on his status after the boyfriend was a dead end."

It felt as if the whole place grew quiet, which I knew it hadn't. "Her father was the blast from the past who contacted her," I said. "I bet he was the reason she drained her savings as well."

"Why would she give him money?" Georgia asked. "Didn't you say he was in prison since Carrie was a little girl?"

"Maybe he threatened her or her baby if she didn't give him the money he needed," Nikki said.

"Needed for what?" Georgia said.

"I don't know," Nikki said. "He'd just gotten out of prison; he must have needed money."

"Say that's true," Georgia said. "If her dad did come to her for money and she gave it to him, where is she?"

No one said a word.

I looked at Wilder. "Do you know where he is now? Someone must be keeping track of him. Like a parole officer?"

"I spoke to his parole officer today. He said he disappeared a few weeks after he was released. The last tip they had was that he was seen in Mexico, but it was unsubstantiated."

"What now?" I asked. "This feels like a real lead."

"I've already made arrangements to visit the prison where he served his time. I'll talk to other inmates in his block to see if he shared his plans with anyone before he was released."

Chapter 18

The next day seemed to drag on endlessly as I waited for Wilder to call. Initially, I sensed he wasn't going to agree to do it despite my request, but after I badgered him through two beers, he finally agreed, I'm sure just to get me to leave him alone. He'd have to drive to the prison and conduct his interviews, then drive back to Holiday Bay, so I was certain I wouldn't hear from him until late in the day. Needing a distraction, I walked over to the main house to see how Lonnie and his crew were doing. Only a couple more days of work and they'd be off for two weeks for the holiday break.

"Wow, the kitchen is really starting to look like a kitchen," I said after picking my way through the debris at the front of the house.

"Cabinets are in and we'll get the countertops in before we take off for the holiday," Lonnie said. "The doors and windows are in and the painting is done in this room, and the paint and trim is done in both the living room and the game room. I still need to do the tile in the downstairs bathroom, but that won't take long. Might even get it done tomorrow; then all we'll need to do when we get back after New Year's is the flooring and we can move on to the second story."

"It looks fantastic. Better than I even imagined. And you got it done so quickly."

"Hired on some extra labor. Have you decided on colors for the second- and third-floor suites?"

"Not yet. I guess I've been focused on this floor. I'm not sure if I should do them all the same or have a different color scheme for each."

"Just my opinion, but I think I'd create a different feel for each suite. Have you decided about the attic?"

"I'll clear it out at some point after the holiday, but I think I want to create a fifth suite up there as we discussed earlier. In fact, we may use the manager's suite as a rental and Georgia may stay in the cottage, at least for a while. We talked about doing theme weekends, and having six suites to rent out would make more sense."

Lonnie nodded. "I like the idea. I've always wanted to attend one of those murder mystery parties."

"If you can find a sitter, I'll comp a suite for you and Lacy when we do our first one."

"For that we'll find a sitter. Might have to divide the kids up into manageable groups if it's going to be a whole weekend, but I'm sure Lacy's mom would watch Maddie and her sister would take the twins. I have a cousin in town who would probably watch Sadie and the boys. Just give me plenty of notice so I can get everyone lined up."

"Do you have a lot of family in the area?"

Lonnie smiled. "A bunch. Sometimes it feels like too much, but other times it feels just right."

Georgia was in town this morning, so it was a lot quieter when I got back to the cottage than I was used to. I thought about taking Ramos for a walk and had actually gone into my bedroom to find my heavy boots when my cell rang. It was Wilder.

"So?" I asked. "Did you find out what Carrie's dad might be up to?"

"Maybe."

"Are you driving? It sounds like you're on speaker."

"Yeah, I'm heading back. I'll be in the office in thirty minutes. It might be easier to talk in person if you want to meet me in town."

"I'll head your way. I should be there by the time you get back."

After I hung up, I looked at my phone. Had Chief Colt Wilder just invited me to his office to discuss an ongoing investigation? I had to admit I was surprised. When we'd talked the previous evening, he hadn't even wanted to call me about his findings. At least not at first. Although we'd had a lot of fun. Once he began to relax, I could see he was an interesting guy with a wonderful sense of humor. I hadn't noticed that before, but last night was the first time I'd talked to him in a social situation. Not only had he been relaxed and entertaining, he'd been downright charming.

I pulled on my jacket and took Ramos out for a quick bathroom break, then texted Georgia to let her know where I was going in case she came home while I was in town. I fed and watered both animals, then headed to my SUV.

I'd thought I'd beat Wilder to his office, but when I pulled into the lot, I saw his cruiser in front of the building.

"Afternoon, Peach," I said.

"Afternoon, Abby. He said to go on back."

"Thanks. By the way, I love your window display. Very festive."

Peach smiled. "Why, thank you. I did take some time with it."

I made my way down the hallway to Wilder's office. The door was open, but I rapped on the doorframe anyway. Wilder was on the phone, but he looked up, smiled, then gestured me in. I sat down on one of the chairs across the desk from him just as he was signing off.

"That was Carl Sandman of the FBI," Wilder said.

"The FBI? Are they part of this now?"

"He's an old friend who's looking in to a few things for me. I spoke to a cellmate of Griff Murphy, Carrie's father, who informed me that Murphy had plans to look up his old boss after he was released. We suspect he was referring to Mickey Boyle."

"Who is he?" I asked.

"A crime boss who operates out of the Boston area. Murphy was convicted twenty years ago for his part in a munitions sale gone bad. Five men died in the ensuing shootout. Murphy was shot but lived."

"So how does Boyle fit into this?"

"It's long been suspected Murphy was involved in the arms sale on behalf of Boyle, although he never admitted it."

"Okay, wait, so Carrie's father's name is Griff Murphy but Carrie's last name is Long. Did she change it?"

"Her mother changed it to her maiden name after her father was arrested."

"Makes sense. So what does this have to do with Carrie?"

"I'm not sure. At least not yet. But after I spoke to Murphy's cellmate, I did some checking. I located a very heavily guarded estate about forty miles north of here, belonging to the Boyle family. It was handed down to some cousins after Mickey's grandfather passed away. The FBI has been surveying the place and has video footage of a man fitting Murphy's description entering the compound two months ago with a woman fitting Carrie's description. It's a long shot, but my gut tells me that Carrie somehow got involved in whatever her father was in to and may be held on the estate."

"You need to go get her."

"I'm not doing anything. The FBI is working with the ATF, who supposedly has an undercover agent inside. If we can confirm Carrie is being held, we'll figure out a way to get her out. Until then, I wait."

Wait? Okay. I could do that. Wilder was right; there was nothing I could do other than wait. Still, to be so close to finding the girl who'd been haunting my dreams and not know for certain was killing me. "How long do you think it will take?"

"To find out whether Carrie is alive and still inside, not that long. The ATF has initiated communications protocol with their agent. If we can confirm that Carrie is both alive and being held on the estate, I'll wait for the ATF to come up with a plan to get her out. That could take a bit longer."

"Yes, okay, I guess you wouldn't want to just storm the place with guns blazing."

Wilder grinned. "No, that wouldn't be the best plan."

I sat back in my chair, considering the man across from me. "Why did you invite me here?"

"Containment."

"Containment?"

"I knew you'd be waiting for my call, and if I told you what I'd found out over the phone, you might take it upon yourself to do something rash."

I raised a brow. "Rash? Me? Why would you think that?"

Wilder chuckled. "My FBI buddy is friends with your FBI buddy. I've actually been dialed in on some fairly amusing stories."

I actually felt my face turn red. I was going to kill Mike when I next saw him. "That was when I was in college. I'm not a kid any longer. I understand it's best to think before diving into the deep end. Despite my earlier statement, I don't even have a gun to use to storm the compound. Well, that isn't true. I have Ben's gun. But it isn't even loaded. I don't think. I'm actually not sure. But it's locked away in the lockbox where he kept it." I took a deep breath. "I'm babbling. I'm sorry. I'm not usually a babbler. For some reason, I'm really nervous." I looked Wilder in the eye. "Is that weird?"

Wilder smiled a little half smile. "It's not weird. You've been drawn into the mystery of Carrie Long and you've grown to care about her even though you've never met her. I find it admirable and charming. I think we're both hoping she'll be found and that she's okay. The waiting's never easy."

"I'm not a great waiter. I tend to be more of a doer."

"Which is a good thing," Wilder said. "Do you have any idea how bad I feel that Carrie may be alive and I'd all but given up on looking for her?"

"You didn't know. It did seem as if she took off, as everyone said."

"You didn't believe that and you didn't even know her."

I bobbed my head. "True, but maybe not knowing her gave me an advantage. I'm sure you did the best you could with the information you had."

Wilder shook his head. "No. I really didn't. I had a personal crisis going on at the time Carrie went missing, and I let that affect my judgment. When the detective from the county told me that they'd determined she'd most likely taken off, I shouldn't have gone along with his determination. If she's been held all this time and something happens to her, I'll never forgive myself."

I wanted to ask what sort of personal crisis he'd been experiencing but decided not to. At least not at this point. I could ask Lacy about it later.

We both jumped when Wilder's phone rang.

"Wilder."

I held my breath as his frown turned into a smile. "Excellent. I'll head over now."

I stared at Wilder after he hung up. "Is she there? In the compound?"

"She was. The undercover agent managed to get her out. She's on her way to a safe house. I've been asked to pick up the baby and the aunt and bring them there."

I couldn't help but grin. "Can I come along?"

Wilder shrugged. "Sure. I don't see why not."

Chapter 19

It was almost noon by the time I managed to pull myself out of bed the next morning. Of course, I hadn't gotten home until the wee hours of the morning. I pulled Rufus into my arms and hugged him to my chest. Tears streamed down my face as I remembered the moment when mother and baby were reunited. I think I was sobbing harder than anyone, and I'm still not sure if my tears were of joy for them or of sorrow that I would never be reunited with my own sweet little baby.

I could hear Georgia in the kitchen. She was still waiting to be filled in on the details. I could hear voices, so I suspected Nikki was there too. I flipped back the covers and headed into the shower. It had been a very long time since I'd shed as many tears as I had in the past twelve hours. I was sure my face was a mess. Hopefully, a long shower and a lot of makeup would hide the turmoil I was still feeling.

I stayed in the shower until the water ran cold, then pulled on a pair of black leggings and a bright red sweatshirt, fixed my face the best I could with the little bit of makeup I owned, plastered a smile on my face, and wandered out for the cup of coffee I hoped was waiting for me.

"There she is," Georgia said with a smile on her face and an extra-large mug of coffee in her hands. "Nikki and I have been dying for you to wake up so we could hear all about it."

I took a long sip of coffee, then slid onto one of the barstools. "I appreciate you letting me sleep. If the roles had been reversed, I'm not sure I would have let you sleep."

Nikki laughed. "So tell us everything. Start at the beginning."

I started off with the phone call from Wilder, asking me to meet him at his office, then segued into the theory about the compound, the FBI footage that showed Carrie enter it, and the undercover agent who located her and managed to sneak her out. I also filled them in on what had happened in the safe house.

"I bet she was so happy to see her baby," Georgia gushed.

I felt tears prick in my eyes but fought them back. "It really was an amazing and emotional reunion," I said. "Very heartwarming. I can't imagine the hell that poor woman must have been going through, not knowing if she would ever see her baby again."

"It must have been awful," Nikki said.

Georgia sent me a soft smile. I knew she understood the mixed emotions I'd been juggling.

"How did she end up in the compound?" Nikki asked.

I took another sip of my coffee. "Prior to his arrest, Carrie's father, Griff Murphy, worked for a crime boss named Mickey Boyle. Murphy was involved in an arms sale that went bad, and a bunch of people died. He was sent to prison for twenty years. Shortly before he was released, he told a cellmate he planned to look up his old boss, which he did. The boss, however, was less than thrilled to see him. It was Boyle's belief that Murphy had hidden away money that belonged to him. He wanted it back and threatened to kill Griff, Carrie, and her daughter if he didn't retrieve the money and return it. Griff went to Carrie and told her all their lives depended on him getting money to give to Boyle. Carrie didn't have as much money as he wanted, but her dad convinced her that she had enough to serve as a down payment and he would get the rest. He also promised that if she gave him the money, he would disappear from her life forever."

"So she drained her account and arranged to meet up with him," Nikki provided.

"Exactly," I answered. "The meeting was for the day after she went missing but, according to Carrie, her father showed up at her home late that night, saying he needed the money right then. Carrie had hidden the money in her locker at the market, so she called her neighbor to sit with the baby and then went there with her father in her car. Carrie often opened the store, so she had a key and the combination to the alarm. She told her dad to wait for her and went in to get the cash. When she returned, there was another car in the lot. Inside it were two men with guns. One of them got into the back seat of her car and told her to drive. He directed her to the compound."

"And they held her there all this time?" Georgia said. "Why?"

"Carrie still isn't sure. She was separated from her father as soon as they arrived. She never saw him again. She thinks he's probably dead. They showed her to a nice room with a private bath and told her to wait. She had no choice, so she waited, but no one ever came to get her. Women brought her food and drink and saw to her needs, but they wouldn't give her any information. She was basically locked in the room all this time. She said it seemed as if they'd forgotten about her. Wilder's FBI friend thought they probably just didn't know what to do with her. She'll stay in the safe house with her baby and aunt until it's all right for her to return to Holiday Bay."

"Do you think it will ever be all right?" Nikki asked.

"Wilder said he wouldn't be surprised if she had to remain in protective custody for the rest of her life. It's too soon to tell. The FBI made the decision to pull the undercover agent out of the compound after he helped Carrie escape, so there's no one on the inside to tell them what's going on or how Boyle responded to the news that Carrie's gone."

"Wow," Nikki said.

Wow is right. Talk about a crazy end to what was already a very complex story. One thing was certain: My next book was going to practically write itself. I was already outlining chapters in my mind.

"So, it looks like we actually had four separate mysteries rather than just one," Georgia said. "The case of the boxes in the basement, the case of Carrie Long's disappearance, the case of Darcy Jared's murder, and Karen Stinson's accident. At least I'm assuming it was an accident."

I frowned. "I guess. The only reason it was considered to be something other than an accident was because of the connection between her and the other girls." Even as I said it, I knew in my heart the story of Karen Stinson wasn't over yet.

Chapter 20

"Oh look. I think we have a search-and-rescue cat." Nikki laughed, clapping her hands when Rufus came trotting into the living room with the stuffed doggy Tanner had hidden for the five dogs in training he had living with him to find. It was Christmas Eve, and Nikki and Tanner had invited Georgia and me, along with Rufus and Ramos, to dinner. I was hesitant to bring Rufus after Nikki informed me that the five dogs in training would be included in the celebration, but Rufus seemed to have no problem taking control, bossing them around the way he'd been bossing Ramos for weeks.

"Well, I'll be damned," Tanner said. "I've never seen a cat do that before."

"He's a smart cat," I said. "And he knows what he wants and how to get it."

"It's true," Georgia said. "He bosses Ramos around all day long and he doesn't seem to mind."

Rufus trotted over to Tanner and dropped the toy at his feet. Then he sat down and stared at him.

"He's waiting for his treat," Nikki said. "You did tell the dogs that whichever one of them found the stuffed toy would get a treat."

"I don't think he'll want a dog treat," Tanner replied. He looked at the buffet table, where Maria was setting out their meal. "Maybe a small piece of prime rib."

In the end, all the animals, including Ramos and Tanner's five dogs in training, were given prime rib out on the enclosed porch. Tanner had just returned from washing up after feeding the animals when a car pulled into the drive. "That must be Colt," Tanner said. "I was hoping he'd be here in time to eat."

I hadn't known he was coming, but I was happy he had. His comment about a personal tragedy had been on my mind since he'd made it. I still didn't know what it had been, but I did know Christmas Eve was a night to be with family and friends, not alone with a microwave dinner.

Once Colt was thoroughly welcomed by all, Tanner instructed us to take seats at the long table someone had taken an awful lot of care to set just right. I was happy to see that Maria was going to join us for the meal. When everyone was seated, Tanner stood and raised his glass.

"To friends. Some new and some not so new. May the joy we share at this table tonight see each and every one of us into the new year."

Everyone clinked glasses.

Maria announced we should all serve ourselves buffet style. Once our plates were full, we returned to the table, where Tanner was busy pouring wine. Not only was the house beautifully decorated, but everyone seemed to be relaxed and happy. After the year Georgia and I and probably Colt had had, that in and of itself seemed like a miracle.

"I'm glad you made it," I said to Colt when we returned to the table.

"I would have been here earlier, but I went by the safe house to bring gifts to Carrie and her daughter."

A warmth spread through me. "That was so nice of you."

"I figured a safe house wasn't the best place to spend the holiday, although they seemed perfectly happy to be there. I convinced the agent staying with them to allow Velma to come over with a meal."

"Velma is with them as well?"

"She is. I know it isn't protocol, but she really wanted to see Carrie and Carrie really wanted to see her. I convinced the agent we could trust her not to give Carrie's secret away."

I placed my hand over Colt's. "You're a good guy, Colt Wilder."

"We'll see if you feel that way the next time I tell you to stay out of my cases," he said with a laugh.

I raised a brow. "I'm not worried about that. You seem like a smart guy. Seems to me your cases are exactly where you'd want me to be."

"Are you trying to tell me that you're an author by day and a mystery-solving superhero by night?"

I winked. "Absolutely."

Up Next From Kathi Daley Books

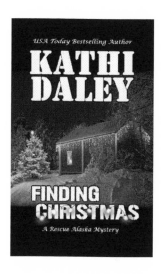

https://amzn.to/2JEZP9W

Preview

Saturday, December 15

The short days of winter had set in, creating a state of almost perpetual darkness. When combined with the heavy clouds that had blanketed the area for the past week, I was beginning to think the sun had disappeared completely. Having lived in Rescue, Alaska, my entire life, I'd learned to roll with the changing weather, but for some reason, this year the endless snow and dark skies were beginning to get on my nerves. Not that there was a thing I could do about the weather, I reminded myself as I handed out event tickets to the sugared-up children at the annual Winter Wonderland Christmas Celebration.

"You do realize that since we've been here, Grandma has been run over by a reindeer at least three times, Frosty has stolen some poor guy's hat at least twice, Rudolph has been bullied by his nasally unimpaired classmates a whopping six times, and the Grinch has stolen Christmas despite the fact that my own powers of observation tell me Christmas is alive and well."

I glanced at my ticket booth partner, Officer Hank Houston. He hadn't wanted to participate in this annual event when I'd first approached him about it, but over time, my tenacious nagging had worn him down and he'd agreed to help me with the shift my best friend, Chloe Rivers, had badgered me into signing up for. "I take it you aren't a fan of the kiddie carols Chloe put on an endless loop from hell."

Houston ran his hands through his thick brown hair. "It's not that I have anything against the carols per se, it's just that Christmas isn't really my thing. I guess all the ho-ho-hos and one-horse open sleighs are getting to me. How long is this shift?"

"Four hours."

"And how long have we been here?"

"One hour."

I tried unsuccessfully to suppress a smile as Houston let out a very unmanly groan.

"You sound like you're dying." I chuckled. "It really isn't that bad."

"Isn't it?"

I raised a brow. "Okay, this is a bit much, but I'm going to go out on a limb and assume it isn't just the noise and the chaos. I'd say there's a deep psychological reason you aren't a fan of the jolly old man in red."

Houston shrugged. "It's not that I'm a Grinch, but I'll admit the big guy and I have had a few problems over the years."

"I see. Do you want to talk about it?"

"Not really. Are you sure you need me to help you? It's my day off, barring any emergencies, and it seems like you have it this under control."

I was debating whether to let Houston off the hook when I noticed the very real pain in his eyes. Maybe he really wasn't being a Grinch. I knew he'd moved to Rescue the previous spring after having suffered a personal tragedy he was unwilling to talk about. Now, if I had to guess, that tragedy was

Christmas involved, given his lack of enthusiasm for the holiday. "I get the aversion to the hoopla," I said with compassion. "I haven't always been the biggest lover of the season myself."

Houston frowned. "I'm sorry. I remember you mentioning your parents died in a car accident at Christmas."

I shrugged. "I'm fine. I've mostly been able to move past it." That wasn't totally true, but I liked to tell myself it was.

Houston opened his mouth as if to reply when a woman dressed as an elf came over to us. "Are you Harmony Carson?"

"I am," I answered.

"I have a message for you from a man named Jake Cartwright."

Jake was my boss and brother-in-law. "I wonder why he didn't just call my cell." I pulled it out of my pocket and looked at it. No bars.

The elf replied, "The man I spoke to called the landline we set up for this event when he couldn't get hold of your cell. He said the team has been called out on a rescue. He needs you to meet him at the Rescue Inn as soon as you can get there. And he said to bring Yukon." The elf, who must be new in town because I'd never met her and she didn't seem to know who either Jake or I were, glanced at Houston with an appreciative gleam in her eye. "I don't suppose you're Yukon?"

Houston laughed. "Hardly. I'm Hank Houston. Yukon is a dog," He looked at me with what could only be an expression of relief on his face. "It sounds like duty calls. Carl is on shift today, but a search-

and-rescue call sounds like something I should handle personally."

I found I had to agree. Carl Flanders and Donny Quinlan, the deputies Houston had inherited when he'd taken on the job as police chief, weren't exactly the most motivated men in the world. They provided somewhat adequate support when it came to day-to-day tasks, but they certainly weren't the men you'd want in charge during an emergency, which, if you thought about it, was pretty ironic given that responding to emergencies was pretty much their entire job description.

I picked up the backpack I used as a purse and nodded at Houston. "If you're coming, grab your stuff. I'm already out of here."

"But you can't both leave," the elf complained as Houston began gathering his own hat, coat, and gloves. "Who'll man the ticket booth?"

I handed the cashbox to the woman who wore little more than green tights and some sort of short red dress that barely covered the tops of her thighs. "I'm sure you can handle things until the next shift gets here in three hours." With that, I grabbed Houston's hand and headed toward the exit before anyone came up with a reason to cause us to stay.

******

The search-and-rescue team had been called out to find an elderly man who'd been staying with his daughter and son-in-law at the Rescue Inn. He hadn't been seen since he went up to bed at nine thirty the previous evening, so we weren't sure how long he'd been out in the snow dressed in nothing but his furry red Santa suit. It was almost eleven a.m. now, and the temperature was hovering around zero. If he'd been out in the cold for more than a couple of hours, I was afraid this was going to be a retrieval operation rather than a rescue.

According to Jake, our victim was a seventy-six-year-old named Nick Clauston. Nick's daughter, Noel Snow, had reported her father missing at around ten fifteen that morning. He hadn't come down to breakfast, but initially, she hadn't worried because he slept late and it wasn't unusual for him to skip breakfast altogether. When he hadn't come downstairs by ten o'clock, she went up to his room to check on him. She found he was gone from his room, as was his red Santa suit. She looked around the inn and its immediate area and when he wasn't found, Mrs. Snow called Carl at the police station, who referred her to Jake. Noel told him she had no idea whether her father had wandered off that morning or during the night, although she suspected it might have been this morning because she didn't think it likely he would leave the inn when it was pitch black outside. I certainly hoped that was the case.

"Jake to Harmony," I heard through the two-way radio I carried as I trudged on snowshoes through drifts of deep snow. My search-and-rescue dog Yukon and I had been paired with fellow S&R team member Wyatt Forrester.

I paused, wiping a huge snowflake from my cheek before I answered. "Go for Harmony."

"Sitka seems to have lost the scent." Jake, who served as the leader of the search-and-rescue team, referred to our lead S&R dog. "At first, it seemed like he had something, but now he just looks confused. Do you and Yukon have anything?"

"It seemed Yukon had a scent when we first started out, but he seems to have lost it as well," I answered. I looked around at the dense forest. "It's snowed quite a bit in the past few hours. If the man came this way, it's likely his tracks will be covered."

"Any luck making a connection?"

"No." I looked around at the blanket of white. "I'll try again." The team depended on my ability to psychically connect to victims I was meant to help rescue. My ability, which I oftentimes considered a curse, had come to me during the lowest point in my life. My sister Val, who had become my guardian after our parents died, had gone out on a rescue. She'd become lost in a storm, and although the team tried to find her, they came up with nothing but dead ends. She was the first person I connected to, and the one I most wanted to save. I couldn't save Val, but since then, I'd used my gift to locate and rescue dozens of people.

I found a large rock, brushed off the snow, and sat down. I focused in on the photo of the white-haired man with rosy red cheeks dressed in a very authentic-looking Santa costume. His daughter had told us they'd come to Rescue so her husband could ski, but ultimately, they'd chosen Alaska as their vacation destination so her father could participate in the Santa Festival being held in Tinseltown, only a short drive from Rescue. Well, it was a short drive by Alaska standards. It was a little more than an hour away.

Mrs. Snow had explained that Mr. Clauston suffered from the early stages of dementia, although he seemed to be having a lot of good days lately, and she felt he was doing much better than he was when he was first diagnosed. She had real hope the progression of his disease had been stalled, at least until she'd discovered he'd wandered away without his snow boots or heavy jacket.

I closed my eyes and focused on the man's jolly face. I tried to think as he would, which I hoped would increase my odds of making a connection. Mrs. Snow had told us that at times, her father actually believed he was Santa Clause and behaved accordingly. He'd do things that in his mind Santa would do. For example, not long ago, her father had collected a bunch of stuff he had around his house, wrapped it, and broke into houses up and down the block where he lived, delivering gifts.

Making a connection to a person in need of rescue is far from an exact science. Sometimes their image comes through clearly, while at others, it doesn't come through at all. I knew not to force it. I simply let the images that presented themselves caress my mind. I could hear Yukon panting next to me and Wyatt moving around, but I forced my mind to be still and settle down. I pulled up an image of rosy cheeks, faded blue eyes, white hair, a lopsided smile, and a mind filled with the possibility of magic.

"I might have something," I said after a minute of intense concentration. "Although to be honest, the vision is vague. I can't make out any details."

"What are you picking up?" Jake asked through the radio.

"I sense hay. Maybe a barn?"

"I suppose Mr. Clauston might have sought out shelter in a barn," Jake said. "With all the fresh snow, he couldn't have gotten too far from the inn, though, and I can't think of any barns in the immediate area."

"Yeah." I frowned. "The image of the barn doesn't really fit." I took a deep breath and tried to focus deeper. I could sense Yukon was becoming restless at the delay. I was sure Jake, Sitka, and Landon were restless waiting for me to do my thing as well, and that just made me tense and less able to focus.

I thought back to the interview we'd had with Noel Snow when we'd responded to the call. Houston had taken over from Jake, asking the questions one would ask with any missing persons case. Why had the family been visiting Rescue? How long had the man been missing? What might he have been wearing or taken with him? And how might he have left the area? Houston wondered whether Nick Clauston had access to a vehicle or if it was more likely he had set off on foot. When his daughter said he hadn't had access to a vehicle, Houston asked if he might have hitchhiked. She didn't think he would have, and there was very little traffic on the road where the inn was located, so it was most likely he'd remained within walking distance of the inn. The poor woman had been so upset. I wanted to find her father, but other than the faint sense of him being associated with hay, I had nothing.

I was about to give up when a flash of an elderly man with a white beard that reached the middle of his chest brushed across my mind. "I think I have him," I whispered. "I'm still picking up on the barn, but the image is stronger now. There's something else." I focused in. "A sleigh."

"Where?" Jake asked.

I bit my lip. "I'm not sure."

I released the button on the radio and let my hand and body relax. The image I'd captured felt just out of my reach. The vision was more of a flash of insight. I didn't sense the man was frightened or in any immediate danger. In fact, I was pretty sure he was having a jolly good time.

"We did see those sleigh tracks a ways back," Wyatt reminded me after a few minutes.

I opened my eyes. "You're right." I pressed the button on the radio again. "Harmony to Jake."

"Go for Jake."

"Wyatt and I are going to backtrack. We saw sleigh tracks a ways back. We didn't think much about them because Mr. Clauston's daughter didn't mention a sleigh, but I think we should follow them to see where they lead."

"Send me your coordinates and we'll join you."

Wyatt sent Jake the coordinates and we headed back the way we'd come. Once we arrived at the place where we remembered seeing the tracks, I paused to give Yukon the old man's scent. I took the shirt his daughter had provided from the plastic bag I carried it in and prayed he would pick up the trail again. "This is Nick Clauston," I said to Yukon. "Find Nick."

Yukon sniffed the shirt, then began to sniff the air. At first, he didn't seem to have found the scent, but after a few minutes, he headed out.

"How do you think sleigh tracks might fit into his disappearance?" Wyatt asked as we trudged through the deep snow, following Yukon.

"I don't know. Maybe someone found him. Someone in a sleigh. Maybe he couldn't remember where he was supposed to be, so the person in the sleigh took him back to their barn."

Wyatt looked doubtful. "If you found a man wandering around in the snow dressed in a Santa suit who couldn't remember where he was supposed to be, wouldn't you call the police?"

I let out a breath. "Yeah, I guess I would. I have no idea how the sleigh or barn fit. That's just what came to me when I focused on Mr. Clauston."

Wyatt and I continued to trudge along. It was difficult to walk with so many drifts, so we leaned forward and looked at the ground directly in front of us as we made our way. Eventually I heard Wyatt say, "Yukon is alerting." He walked forward a bit more. "It looks like he found the tracks we saw earlier."

I radioed Jake that we were back to the point we were looking for, and he radioed for us to wait. He and Landon were only a minute or two away from us. I used the wait time to catch my breath. Walking the rough terrain in snowshoes large enough to provide traction in deep snow wasn't an easy task.

Once the other team caught up with us, we slowly made our way forward, trying our best to follow tracks that disappeared into drifts only to reappear again on the other side.

At one point, Wyatt stopped and knelt down for a closer look. We were somewhat protected from the wind here, so the drifts weren't as deep. "There are hoofprints in the snow as well as sleigh tracks, but there aren't any horse prints."

I walked over to where he was standing. It did look like a sleigh pulled by an animal had been through here. "Caribou," I said after studying the two distinct toes.

Wyatt chuckled. "So, you're saying a man dressed in a Santa suit was picked up in a sleigh pulled by reindeer."

I smiled in return. "That's what the evidence suggests." The dogs seemed to have picked up a scent and gone on ahead. Eventually, they stopped walking and looked around. I paused to study the tracks left in the snow. "A sleigh pulled by caribou definitely traveled through here. It seems the sleigh tracks end at the edge of the forest."

"Maybe Santa's magic reindeer took flight once they came to the edge of the meadow," Wyatt teased.

My lips curled into a half smile. "Again, that would seem to be what the evidence suggests."

"I'm sure if we try hard enough, we can come up with an explanation based in reality," Landon countered.

"Perhaps." I took several steps into the woods at the edge of the clearing. I paused, listened, and looked around. I had the distinct feeling we were being watched, but I didn't see or hear anything.

"Do you sense something?" Jake asked.

I shook my head. "I don't know. I feel something, but I'm not sure it's him. I think maybe…" I was cut off by the sound of Jake's phone.

Jake lifted a finger to quiet me so he could answer. "Jake here." Jake raised a brow. "Really? Well, thanks for letting us know." Jake hung up and turned toward us. "It seems Nick is back at the inn."

I narrowed my gaze. "How did he get there?"

"No one's sure. Houston went outside to get something from his squad car and found Nick sitting on the porch swing near the front door. When he asked him where he'd been and how he'd gotten back to the inn, Mr. Clauston told Houston he woke up during the night and saw lights in the sky. He went outside to take a look and got lost. He was just starting to get worried when Santa appeared in a sleigh pulled by two reindeer. He offered to give him a ride home, but when he couldn't remember where home was, Santa took him to his reindeer barn. He gave him a cup of cocoa and a warm blanket and talked to him a bit. Eventually, Mr. Clauston remembered the inn, and Santa brought him back and dropped him off."

"Hot damn," Wyatt said. "I knew Santa was involved in this."

"There's no such thing as Santa," Landon argued.

"I think it's likely the man was hallucinating," Jake said.

"I might agree if not for the sleigh tracks and the reindeer hooves," I countered. "Maybe Wyatt's right. Maybe Mr. Clauston really *was* rescued by Santa."

Jake rolled his eyes. "This is northern Alaska. A lot of people have sleighs, and a fair number have domesticated caribou. I'm sure what he saw were the northern lights and the Santa who picked him up was a Good Samaritan out for a sleigh ride."

"Who, other than Santa of course, goes for a sleigh ride in the middle of the night?" I queried.

"Yeah, who?" Wyatt laughed.

Jake started walking back the way we'd come. I didn't actually believe Mr. Clauston had been saved by Santa, but it was fun messing with Jake and Landon, who were so steadfast in their disbelief. I didn't know who had saved him; I was just glad he was okay.

******

After we returned to the inn, Jake spoke to Nick's daughter, while Wyatt, Landon and I, gathered our stuff and began loading the trucks. I had to admit that Marty and Mary Miller, the owners of the inn, had done a wonderful job decorating. Not only was the outside of the building decked out in lights, but the interior of the cozy lodging had been strung with lights and garland as well. I could see why the place was so popular with the holiday crowd. Staying at the Inn must be a bit like spending the holiday at Santa's magical workshop.

"The place looks nice," Landon said, as he passed the spot where I'd paused to admire the fifteen foot tree.

"It's really beautiful," I answered and I stuffed down a longing in my heart. "Before she died, my mom used to decorate a tree much like this one. I can still remember the colorful lights and the whisper of Christmas as I curled up on the floor looking up through the branches."

"It sounds nice," Landon replied, as I continued to gaze upon the tree.

I sighed as the memories came flooding forth. "It was magical. My mom really understood the importance of the season and she worked hard to make everything perfect. At times, when I allow my mind to drift into the past, I can almost hear the carols on the stereo; smell the pinesap from the tree; and see the shiny red bulbs reflecting my image, as I waited for Santa."

Landon took a step closer and put his arm around my shoulder. He gave my arm a squeeze as we stood in silence and continued to view the tree. White lights twinkled and danced like stars on a clear winter night. I let out a soft breath as I rested my head his shoulder. "I love the pinecones that have been strategically placed around the bright red bulbs and white lights to give the tree an outdoorsy feel."

"Have you put up a tree yet this year?" Landon asked.

I took a slight step away and shook my head. It really wasn't like me to be quite so sappy. Practical, I reminded myself, was more my style. "I thought about it but I really don't have extra cash to buy decorations and a tree without decorations will really be nothing more than an invitation for the dogs to pee on it and the cats to climb it."

Landon's eyes grew large as if a lightbulb suddenly went on. "Your decorations were stored in the barn."

I nodded. "I didn't have a lot to begin with but the decorations I did have were in the barn when it burned. It's fine though. Jake went crazy decorating the bar this year so I figure I can get my Christmas jollies while I am at work."

I turned back toward the front door. "I'll grab Yukon. Jake looks like he is almost done talking to Marty and Mary and I'm sure he'll want to get on with our own debriefing."

Landon nodded, and picking up the backpack with the supplies we'd brought with us, he headed out to Jake's truck. I had picked up my own Jeep when I'd gone home to get Yukon so I decided to drop Yukon back at home before meeting Jake and the others at Neverland. Once I'd dropped him off, I headed to the bar to meet the others.

"Other than the Santa factor, does anyone have anything to add that may prove to be unique to this case? Anything we might want to keep in mind for future rescues?" Jake asked the standard question he asked during every debriefing even though this rescue had turned out to be pretty tame.

Everyone agreed that nothing out of the ordinary had occurred and we all conveyed the fact that we were just happy that Nick had been returned to the inn in one piece however it was that he managed to get there.

Once Jake had asked all the questions needed for the report, I headed over to the Rescue Alaska Animal Shelter. The gang planned to decorate that day and I didn't want to miss the party. By the time I arrived, Harley Medford, founder and benefactor for the shelter, had already hung the lights along the roofline. The red and white lights against the white snow and dark gray sky gave the place a festive feel which did a lot to chase away the ho-hums that I'd been experiencing as of late.

"It looks great." I walked over and stood next to Serena Walters, shelter volunteer, who was holding the ladder and handing Harley, who was wearing a fuzzy Santa hat, C9 replacement bulbs.

"When Harley Medford does Christmas, Christmas knows it has been done," Harley chuckled.

I rolled my eyes. "For someone who makes a living delivering the perfect line at the perfect time that was really corny."

Harley laughed as he screwed the white light into the empty socket next to the red bulb. "Maybe, but you have to admit the place is looking pretty festive."

Harley climbed down the ladder then stood back to admire his work.

"It really does look fantastic," I said as we admired the red and white lights. "And the Santa on the roof with the eight dogs pulling the sleigh is adorable. Where did you get them anyway?"

"Special order. I wanted the shelter to really stand out. The lights are great but the sleigh with the dogs gives the place character, as well as identity."

"Well I for one am impressed. If I had to guess at this point I'd say we have a very good chance at winning the competition the chamber is hosting."

"That's the plan." Harley crossed his arms and gazed at the building. "I still need to put lights around the windows and I don't want to forget the wreaths I picked up in town." Harley turned and headed toward his truck. Serena and I tagged along behind. It was less than two weeks until Christmas and the whole town of Rescue had gone just a bit Christmas crazy. It had started when Jake had gone all out decorating Neverland and other businesses around town decided to try to outdo his efforts. The end result was that the first ever Rescue Alaska decorating war had been born. Not to be outdone, the gang at the animal shelter had decided we needed to put up our own decorations. Luckily Harley had announced that he was all in and not only agreed to provide the funds to buy the decorations we'd need but the labor to help put them up as well.

"So how did the rescue go?" Harley asked.

"It went well. It turned out that the man who thought he was Santa was rescued by the man who actually is Santa."

"The man who actually is Santa?" Serena asked, as Harley began handing her wreathes to carry.

I took a minute and filled Harley and Serena in on the entire story.

"That is kind of fun in a ten days before Christmas sort of way." Serena's eyes danced with merriment when she spoke.

"That's what Wyatt and I thought. Of course Landon and Jake were all practical with the 'there is no such thing as Santa' bit."

"Of course. That isn't surprising. Landon especially is Mr. Logic," Serena said.

"As fun as the thought of the real Santa rescuing a lost man dressed as Santa is, I do wonder who actually rescued him," Harley said. "It seems a little odd that this good samaritan just dropped him off at the inn and didn't bring him inside."

I frowned as Harley loaded me up with wreathes as well. "I guess it is a little odd. Nick was obviously confused. It seems that whomever brought him back to the inn would want to make sure he was safe with someone who would look out for him."

"Unless it really was Santa and he didn't want to blow his cover," Serena giggled. "Speaking of Santa did you volunteer at the Christmas Festival as you planned?"

"For a while," I answered. "I had a four hour shift but was called in on the rescue after just one hour."

"How was it?" Serena asked.

"Fun in an overdone sort of way."

Serena raised a brow. "Overdone?"

"It was just a lot. A lot of people, a lot of decorations, a lot of music, and a lot of food. I think that generally speaking everyone was having fun though. Are you still volunteering tomorrow?"

Serena smiled. "I am. And I'm really looking forward to it."

"I never did get around to signing up for a volunteer shift," Harley said. "But I would like to attend. Is it going on all weekend?"

"Until five o'clock tomorrow," I confirmed.

"I don't suppose you want to come along and show me around?" Harley asked.

I shrugged. "Sure. I can do that. Just let me know what time you want to go."

"I'll text you."

I set the last load of wreaths on the reception desk and stood back to take it all in. The shelter was going to be more festively decorated than the actual North Pole if Harley had his way about it.

"It looks like the couple who are adopting that malamute we took in last week are here," Serena said after she set the wreaths in her arms on the counter next to mine. "I'll go and talk to them. Be sure to save a few of these wreaths for the reception area."

"We should string lights inside as well," I added, as Serena walked away.

"There are boxes of lights in the office," Serena said over her shoulder.

I picked up one of the wreaths and began tying on a red bow from the spool of thick red ribbon Harley had brought. "Maybe we should wrap the front door like a present. It might get ruined if we have a big wind, but the door is protected from all but a direct northerly wind and it would look festive."

"It seems someone has found the Christmas Spirit," Harley said. "You didn't seem all that enthusiastic about decorating when Serena first suggested it last week."

"I was enthusiastic. I was also concerned about the cost and time commitment. But then you stepped up to help. And there is something about a rescue involving Santa that that brings the magic of the season into play."

"Well I for one am happy that the whole team is behind the project." Harley took a step back and looked at the building. "Maybe we need lights in the trees."

"That would look awesome but I'm not sure the electrical system can handle many more lights than we already have."

"True. I guess I'll have to upgrade the electrical system before next year. I bought a generator for the house. Maybe something like that would work for the tree lights."

I shrugged. "If you want to go to all that expense I think it would look awesome."

Harley and I worked side by side until the shelter looked like it might ignite from all the lights. I was just about to suggest we head inside for some hot cocoa when a man in a Chevy Truck pulled up, got out, opened the back door, lifted an adorable yellow puppy who looked to be some sort of lab mix into his arms, and headed toward me.

"Do you work here?" He asked.

"Yes. I'm a volunteer."

The man handed me the puppy, who I estimated to be four months old, turned, and walked back toward his truck.

"Wait," I yelled after him. When the man didn't stop I thrust the puppy into Harley's arms then took off at a jog. "Are you surrendering this puppy?"

The man opened the driver's side door to his truck. "I am."

"Why?"

The man glared at me with angry eyes. "I don't want or need a dog."

"So why did you get a puppy?"

"I didn't get a puppy. My mother was not happy about the fact that I decided to live all alone in this god forsaken wilderness, so she decided to remedy the situation by giving me a forty pound pooping and chewing machine."

I put my hand out to stop the man from leaving before I could have my say. "Puppies chew and poop in the most inopportune places but with a little training…"

The man slipped into the truck. "I'm not interested."

"Do you live here in town?" I wondered.

The man shook his head. "About an hour north of here. Now if you don't mind."

I stood back. The man closed his door and drove away.

I stamped down my anger. Some people! Of course I was glad that the man dropped the puppy off with us and didn't simply abandon it as some folks were apt to do. I watched the truck pull onto the highway and out of sight then turned around and headed back to where the pup was slathering puppy kisses all over Harley's face. "He likes you," I laughed.

"Maybe but that doesn't mean I have room in my life for a dog."

Feigning innocence I replied. "Did I say that I though you would be a good match for this little cutie?"

"No but I know you and I've seen you work your magic on others. First you will point out how cute the little guy is and then you will casually mention how much the pup likes me. Once I agree to that, in theory at least, you will segue into a comment about it being the holidays and the shelter being overcrowded and wouldn't it be nice if the pup had a home for Christmas. I would attempt to extract myself from the situation by pointing out all the very real reasons why a puppy would not work for me given my lifestyle, but eventually I would find myself seduced by your sweet smile and big brown eyes, and before I even knew what had happened, this energetic little chewing machine would be entrenched in my house happily eating my sofa while I tried to figure out how on earth you had talked me into bringing him home in the first place."

I laughed. "Very good. That is exactly what I'd planned. So how about it? Just for a few days until I can find someone to foster him."

"I thought the whole reason you wanted to open this shelter was to house the local animals that had been abandoned."

"It is," I replied. "And you know how much I and everyone values your contribution. But this little guy is just a baby. He needs training and attention. He really would be better off in a home."

Harley hesitated.

"But if you are too busy, I guess I can ask Wyatt or maybe Landon. Neither would be as good a foster as you, but I suppose beggars can't be choosers." I sighed in such a way as to indicate that the situation was a lot direr than it actually was.

Harley let out a long breath. "Okay fine. But just for a few days. I can't have a dog on a permanent basis. I travel all the time. It wouldn't be practical."

"I know. And a few days will help a lot." I stood on tip toe and kissed Harley on the cheek. "Let's head inside. I'll see if I can find a collar and leash and then we will head to the pet store."

"Pet store?"

"The pup is going to need things. Food. A bed. Some toys and grooming supplies. You know, all the standard stuff. Oh and a name. We can't keep calling him the pup."

"I'm not naming him."

I shrugged. "Okay then I will. How about Rudolph."

Harley raised a brow. "Rudolph?"

"It is almost Christmas and the man did say that he lived up north. Rudolph seems like an appropriate name for a Christmas puppy from up north."

Harley held the pup out and took a closer look. "He is going to be a large dog. And I can already tell he is smart. He needs a name with some dignity. How about Brando."

I smiled. It looked like Brando had found a new daddy whether Harley knew it or not.

Cranberry Muffins

Combine in large bowl:
2 cups flour
1 cup sugar
1½ tsp. baking powder
1 tsp. ground nutmeg
1 tsp. ground cinnamon
½ tsp. ground ginger
½ tsp. baking soda
½ tsp. salt

Cut in:
1 stick butter

Add:
¾ cup orange juice
2 eggs, beaten
1 tbs. vanilla extract

Fold in:
1½ cups cranberries, chopped
2 cups pecans, chopped

Bake in greased muffin cups at 375 degrees for about 20 minutes (toothpick should come out clean). Cool.

Books by Kathi Daley

Come for the murder, stay for the romance.

Zoe Donovan Cozy Mystery:

Halloween Hijinks
The Trouble With Turkeys
Christmas Crazy
Cupid's Curse
Big Bunny Bump-off
Beach Blanket Barbie
Maui Madness
Derby Divas
Haunted Hamlet
Turkeys, Tuxes, and Tabbies
Christmas Cozy
Alaskan Alliance
Matrimony Meltdown
Soul Surrender
Heavenly Honeymoon
Hopscotch Homicide
Ghostly Graveyard
Santa Sleuth
Shamrock Shenanigans
Kitten Kaboodle
Costume Catastrophe
Candy Cane Caper
Holiday Hangover
Easter Escapade
Camp Carter
Trick or Treason
Reindeer Roundup
Hippity Hoppity Homicide

Firework Fiasco
Henderson House
Holiday Hostage – *December 2018*

Zimmerman Academy The New Normal
Zimmerman Academy New Beginnings
Ashton Falls Cozy Cookbook

Tj Jensen Paradise Lake Mysteries by Henery Press:

Pumpkins in Paradise
Snowmen in Paradise
Bikinis in Paradise
Christmas in Paradise
Puppies in Paradise
Halloween in Paradise
Treasure in Paradise
Fireworks in Paradise
Beaches in Paradise
Thanksgiving in Paradise – *Fall 2019*

Whales and Tails Cozy Mystery:

Romeow and Juliet
The Mad Catter
Grimm's Furry Tail
Much Ado About Felines
Legend of Tabby Hollow
Cat of Christmas Past
A Tale of Two Tabbies
The Great Catsby
Count Catula
The Cat of Christmas Present
A Winter's Tail

The Taming of the Tabby
Frankencat
The Cat of Christmas Future
Farewell to Felines
A Whisker in Time
The Catsgiving Feast
A Whale of a Tail – *April 2019*

Writers' Retreat Southern Seashore Mystery:
First Case
Second Look
Third Strike
Fourth Victim
Fifth Night
Sixth Cabin
Seventh Chapter
Eighth Witness – January 2019

Rescue Alaska Paranormal Mystery:
Finding Justice
Finding Answers
Finding Courage
Finding Christmas – *December 2018*

A Tess and Tilly Mystery:
The Christmas Letter
The Valentine Mystery
The Mother's Day Mishap
The Halloween House
The Thanksgiving Trip

The Saint Paddy's Promise – *March 2019*

The Inn at Holiday Bay:
Boxes in the Basement
Letters in the Library – *February 2019*

Family Ties:
The Hathaway Sisters
Harper – *February 2019*
Harlow – *May 2019*
Haden – *August 2019*
Haley – *November 2019*

Haunting by the Sea:
Homecoming by the Sea
Secrets by the Sea
Missing by the Sea
Christmas by the Sea – *March 2019*

Sand and Sea Hawaiian Mystery:
Murder at Dolphin Bay
Murder at Sunrise Beach
Murder at the Witching Hour
Murder at Christmas
Murder at Turtle Cove
Murder at Water's Edge
Murder at Midnight

Seacliff High Mystery:
The Secret
The Curse
The Relic

The Conspiracy
The Grudge
The Shadow
The Haunting

Road to Christmas Romance:
Road to Christmas Past

USA Today best-selling author Kathi Daley lives in beautiful Lake Tahoe with her husband Ken. When she isn't writing, she likes spending time hiking the miles of desolate trails surrounding her home. She has authored more than seventy-five books in eight series, including Zoe Donovan Cozy Mysteries, Whales and Tails Island Mysteries, Sand and Sea Hawaiian Mysteries, Tj Jensen Paradise Lake Series, Writers' Retreat Southern Seashore Mysteries, Rescue Alaska Paranormal Mysteries, and Seacliff High Teen Mysteries. Find out more about her books at www.kathidaley.com

Stay up-to-date:

Newsletter, *The Daley Weekly*
http://eepurl.com/NRPDf
Webpage – www.kathidaley.com
Facebook at Kathi Daley Books –
www.facebook.com/kathidaleybooks
Kathi Daley Books Group Page –
https://www.facebook.com/groups/569578823146850/
E-mail – kathidaley@kathidaley.com
Twitter at Kathi Daley@kathidaley –
https://twitter.com/kathidaley
Amazon Author Page –
https://www.amazon.com/author/kathidaley
BookBub –
https://www.bookbub.com/authors/kathi-daley

Made in the USA
Middletown, DE
17 December 2018